WHERE'S WALDO?

THE BOREDOM BUSTER BOOK!

A collection of favorite searches,
games, and activities!

MARTIN HANDFORD

CANDLEWICK PRESS

WELCOME, WALDO-WATCHERS!

COME ALONG WITH ME ON A FIVE-STAR TOUR OF MY
FAVORITE JOURNEYS FROM YEARS GONE BY.

WE'LL HEAD ON VACATION, SAIL THE SEAS, BLAST INTO
OUTER SPACE, TRAVEL BACK IN TIME, THEN SPIN INTO A
WORLD OF MAGIC AND MYSTERY. TO TOP IT ALL OFF,
YOU'RE INVITED TO A TOTALLY TERRIFIC PARTY WITH ALL
MY FRIENDS. HOORAY!

KEEP YOUR BRAIN BUZZING WITH HUNDREDS OF GAMES,
SEARCHES, AND ACTIVITIES. ALONG THE WAY, LOOK OUT
FOR ME AND MY FRIENDS: WOOF (USUALLY ALL YOU CAN SEE
IS HIS TAIL), WENDA, WIZARD WHITEBEARD, AND ODLAW.
KEEP AN EYE OUT FOR OUR FAVORITE THINGS, TOO:

KEY	BONE	CAMERA	SCROLL	BINOCULARS

 BUT THAT'S NOT ALL! YOU'LL FIND TOTALLY
TERRIFIC FIVE-MINUTE CHALLENGES AT THE
BOTTOM OF EVERY PAGE! RACE AGAINST TIME
AND TAKE ON EACH BOREDOM-BUSTING GAME AS QUICKLY
AS YOU CAN.

THERE ARE HOURS OF FUN TO BE HAD, AND THE CLOCK'S
TICKING... SO PICK UP YOUR PENS AND LET'S GO!

GOOD LUCK, THRILL-SEEKERS!

Waldo

TRAVEL ESSENTIALS

Waldo is about to set off on his travels.
Check off everything he is carrying on the list
below, and then find the objects he's missing
in the scene behind him. Bon voyage!

BACKPACK
BALLOON
BELT
BINOCULARS
BUCKET
CAMERA
CLOCK
CUP
FLOWER
MALLET
POM-POM

SATCHEL
SHOVEL
SLEEPING BAG
SNORKEL
SPINNING TOP
TEAPOT
TOP HAT
WALKING STICK

MORE THINGS TO DO
There are some things Waldo can't
travel with! Unscramble the letters
below to find out what he's leaving
behind!

cera rac

dgrna iapno

ckhneti snki

6

Search the background carefully. How many yellow
items of clothing and cool accessories can you see?
Clothing: .... Accessories: ....

COSTUME COSTS

Wenda has given you $15 to spend. You need to buy one or more of each of the items below, but you may buy only one hat. Remember to subtract the discount from the full price. You must spend all of your money!

Hats $3 ($2 off)   Ties $3 ($1 off)

Shirts $10 ($7 off)   Jackets $10 ($6 off)

$____
+ $____
+ $____
+ $____
+ $____
+ $____
$= [15]

$5

$10

MORE THINGS TO DO

* Color in the two large Wenda bills.

* Find twelve other Wenda bills in the scene.

7

FIVE-MINUTE CHALLENGE

You did so well on your first shopping trip that Wenda has given you an extra $10! Work out how many extra of each item you can buy now!

PLANE SNAP

Can you match up the plane playing cards to make eight pairs? Study each one very closely. Chocks away!

8

FIVE-MINUTE CHALLENGE This plane appears on three other pages. Can you find them all? Search fast!

TRAVEL TWISTER

Can you find all the terrific travel words that are
hidden? They go backward, forward, up, and down!

Y	M	T	C	R	L	P	A	S	S	P	O	R	T	O	P
A	R	O	T	T	W	A	E	K	Z	M	K	B	O	D	E
S	U	I	T	C	A	S	E	I	C	L	J	E	N	I	Y
Q	L	W	T	H	K	M	X	W	O	A	G	B	K	L	B
A	W	V	Y	O	F	O	H	R	J	O	U	R	N	E	Y
M	A	S	Z	E	E	D	X	J	S	E	B	B	L	V	N
A	L	C	H	E	P	O	F	I	T	A	O	B	H	A	X
P	K	V	T	A	S	D	N	A	R	B	K	S	B	R	B
A	I	C	R	E	F	L	D	U	W	F	L	N	E	T	P
Q	N	S	A	U	V	A	I	C	A	R	Q	T	A	B	L
D	G	E	D	A	F	W	H	K	L	T	T	R	I	O	A
T	S	S	U	L	B	G	X	J	N	A	W	O	O	F	B
R	T	C	A	M	E	R	A	I	F	K	E	M	A		
A	I	Q	H	V	P	W	X	E	N	A	L	P	B		
I	C	C	L	E	Y	O	S	I	T	F	L	M			
N	K	E	P	B	A	H	C	E	S	Z	A	H			

WORDS TO SEARCH FOR

BOAT • CAMERA • CAR •
JOURNEY • MAP • ODLAW •
PASSPORT • PLANE • SUITCASE
• TRAIN • TRAVEL
• WALKING STICK • WOOF

9

**FIVE-MINUTE
CHALLENGE**

There are more than fifty words you can make with the letters
in ADVENTURE. Work out as many as you possibly can!

DESTINATION EVERYWHERE

Unscramble the letters in the Destination column to spell the names of twelve cities. Then search for flights with "WAL" in them to find out which places Waldo will be traveling to. Wow!

Depart	Destination	Flight	Arrive	Delays
10:00	WEN OYKR	WAL1	22:00	ON TIME
08:00	NOONLD	WDA1	07:00	ON TIME
22:00	GNHO NKGO	WOF1	10:30	1 HOUR
11:30	RASIP	WOF2	21:00	ON TIME
23:00	BUDAI	ODW2	06:00	ON TIME
22:00	AOS AULOP	WAL2	10:00	ON TIME
13:00	STERAMDAM	WZD1	21:00	1 HOUR
21:00	OTONTOR	WZD2	23:00	ON TIME
23:00	KYOTO	WAL4	13:00	ON TIME
10:00	REOM	WAL3	23:00	ON TIME
19:00	SOLO	ODW1	22:00	3 HOURS
07:00	DNEYYS	WDA2	09:00	ON TIME

MORE THINGS TO DO

✳ Did Waldo catch all four flights? Starting with "WAL1," check the arrival time matches the departure time of "WAL2" and so on. Can you also find Wenda's, Woof's, Wizard Whitebeard's, and Odlaw's abbreviated names, where they flew to, and if they caught their flights, too?

FIVE-MINUTE CHALLENGE

Remove two letters and unscramble this text from the board to reveal part of a toe!

WAL ON TIME ....

TRANSPORT TANGLE

At the airport, everyone is in a hurry to refuel!
But which truck is fueling each vehicle?
Follow the lines below to find out!

11

RUNAWAY RUNWAY

Travel from start to finish. You can only go down runways in the direction of the arrows.

START

12

Now try the maze again, but ignore the arrows. Instead, try to find:

• The fastest route
• The longest route

FINISH

MORE THINGS TO FIND

- [ ] A rocket
- [ ] A wind sock
- [ ] A flying ace
- [ ] An open suitcase
- [ ] A French flag
- [ ] Three buckets

13

• A route where you pass
  every single elephant

• A route where you pass
  all the travel crew

LUGGAGE LOOP

There's a lot of chaos going on around this airport conveyor belt! Can you find your way through the luggage tags, lost luggage, and crowds of people to the finish?

Read the instructions before you set off.

- Begin at the start and go forward either one or three squares.

- Move the number of squares as shown— but remember, a red luggage tag takes you backward and a yellow one forward. When you see both, you choose the direction.

- If you land on a square with a single suitcase, move to a matching square and then move forward five squares.

- If you land on a picture square, search for the image in the scene and then move forward five.

FINISH

14

FIVE-MINUTE CHALLENGE

Now that you've looped-the-loop, put on your aviator goggles and take on these flights of fancy:

15

- Match each picture square on the conveyor belt to its character in the scene.
- Count how many passengers are getting off the plane.
- Count how many watches are in the scene. HINT: It's more than twenty.

LOST LUGGAGE

Spot Waldo's lost luggage in these photographs.
Can you find one bag with a red-and-white-striped luggage label,
two bags with white labels, and two bags with blue labels?

MORE THINGS TO FIND

- ☐ A bag with a red luggage label
- ☐ A woman wearing yellow shoes
- ☐ A barrel
- ☐ Seven yellow luggage labels

FIVE-MINUTE CHALLENGE

Unscramble these essentials to see what's in Waldo's bag!
- OTHOT STAPE
- TYDED ERAB
- EAMARC
- RIYAD
- TSSAPM
- GSUSESLASN

TREACHEROUS TRAINS

Something's gone offtrack in this strange station!
Spot ten differences between the two scenes below.

AT THE STATION

AT THE STATION (AGAIN)

Choo-choo-choose the right answer
to this question! The fastest train in
the world travels at:

a) 150 mph
b) 267 mph
c) 210 mph

Then find out which
country it runs in!

STAMPING AROUND

Draw eyes, noses, and mouths to finish the faces in Waldo's stamp collection!

FIVE-MINUTE CHALLENGE

It's coloring chaos! Grab as many coloring supplies as you can, and in five minutes or less:

- Color in all the hats.
- Draw three noses.
- Color in the background of the Waldo stamp.
- Create a funny-patterned beard!

SILLY STAMP SNAP

Now it's time to mail some postcards.
Can you match each postmark to its stamp?

FIVE-MINUTE CHALLENGE

MORE THINGS TO FIND
- [ ] Six balloons
- [ ] A ticklish man
- [ ] An upside-down mummy sarcophagus
- [ ] Someone holding lots of cups
- [ ] A fish fountain

DOG'S DINNER

Cross out all the *W*s to decode Woof's message.
Write the answer in the spaces below each line.
Two *W*s means a break between words.

W O W N W W Y W O U W R W W B W A W R W K W S ,

W W G W E W T W W S W E W T , W W G W O ! W W M W Y W W P W A W L W S

W W A W N W D W W I W W A W R W E W W C W H W A W S W I W N W G

W W O U W R W W F W A W V W O W R W I W T W E

W W T W H W I W N W G W S : W W S W A W U W S W A W G W E W S ,

W W B W O W N W E W S , W W A W N W W D W W C W A W T W S !

MORE THINGS TO FIND

☐ Thirty-one envelopes
☐ A dog that is not wearing a collar
☐ Two blue dog bowls

FIVE-MINUTE CHALLENGE

Decode this message for an extra challenge!
TWUWRWNWWTHWEWWPWAWGWEWWAWNWDWW
FWIWNWDWWAWNWWAWCWCWOWRWDWIWOWN

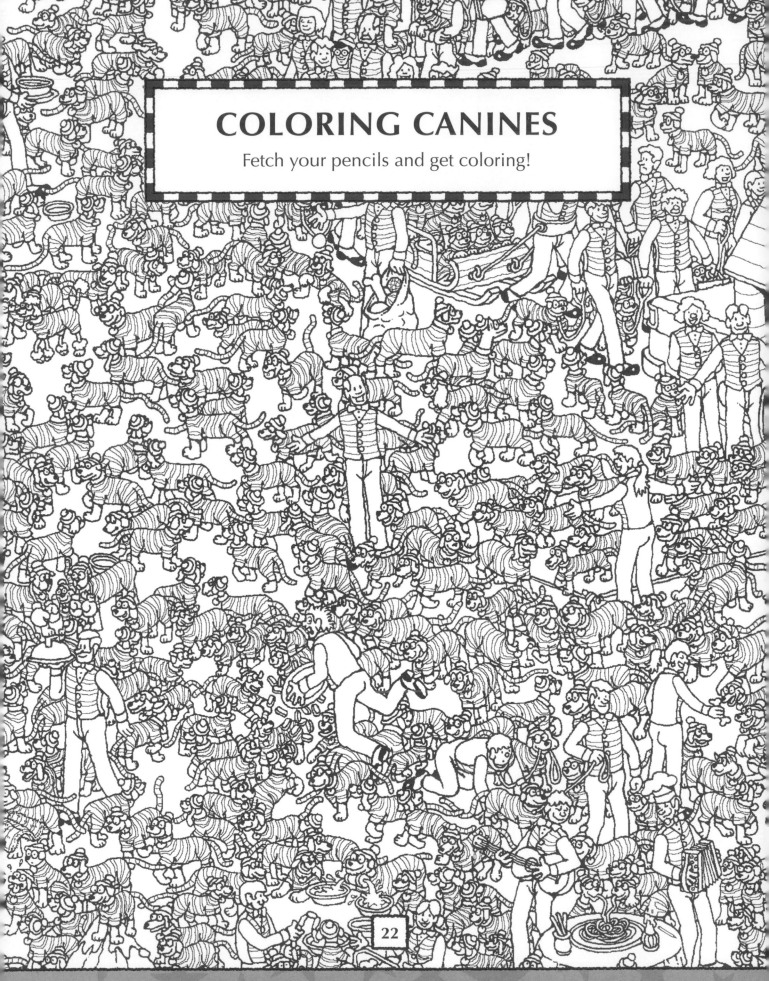

COLORING CANINES
Fetch your pencils and get coloring!

22

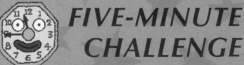

23

☐ Sled dogs
☐ A romantic dinner
☐ A poodle
☐ A guard dog
☐ One Woof being carried!
☐ Doggy masseurs

TO THE TAIL END

Find a way through the maze of Woof tails. Start at the square
with the red tail and use the guide below to help
you reach the square with the white tail.

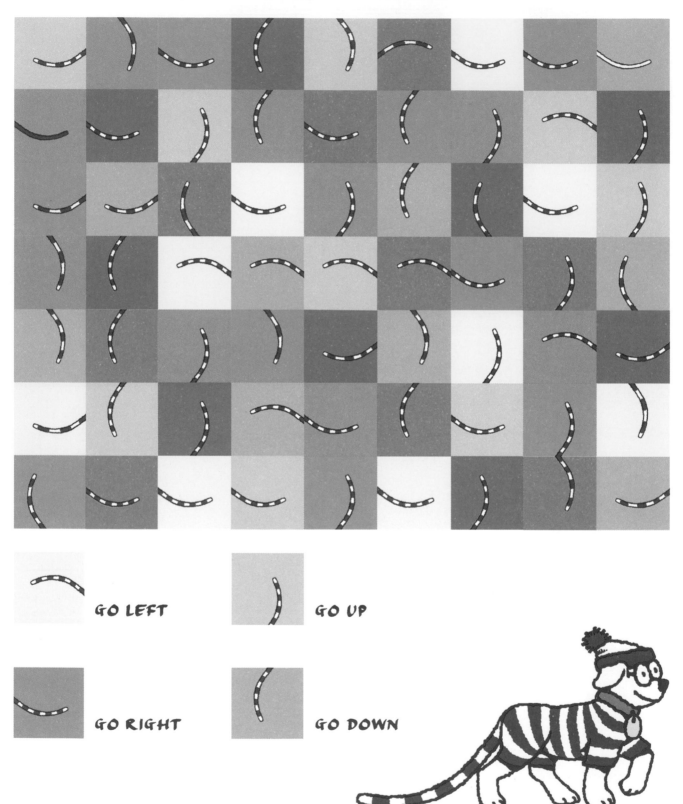

GO LEFT

GO UP

GO RIGHT

GO DOWN

MORE THINGS TO FIND
☐ Eight tails with three white stripes
☐ Twelve tails with four white stripes

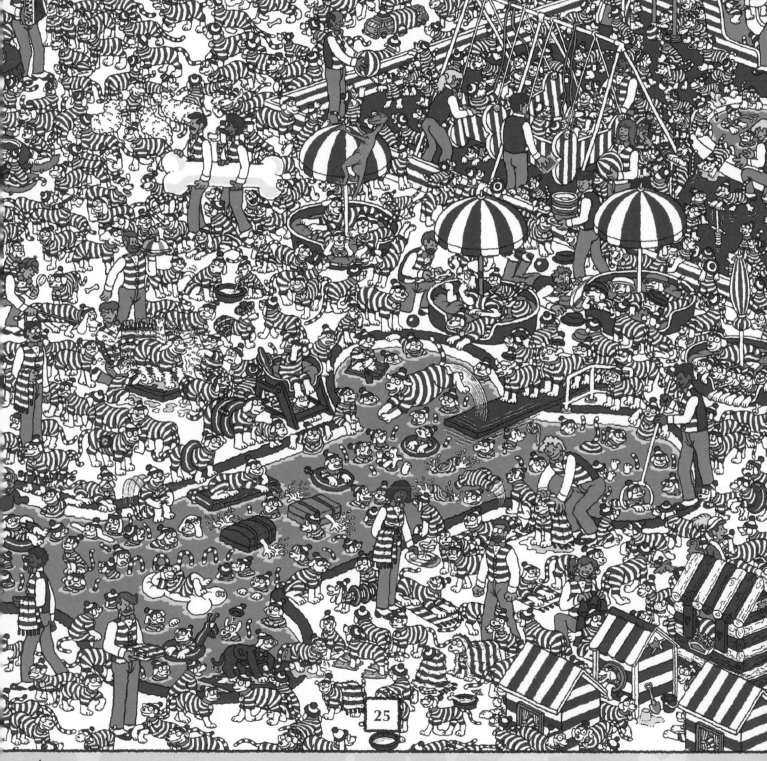

BARE BONES BRAIN BUSTER

Take your time to study this scene closely.
Then turn the page to test your memory.

25

BARE-BONES BRAIN BUSTER

How many of these questions can you answer from memory?
(It's also fun to guess!) Then turn back the page to see how you did.

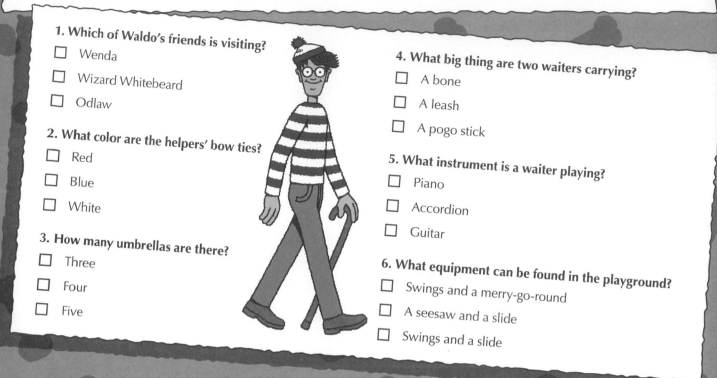

1. Which of Waldo's friends is visiting?
- ☐ Wenda
- ☐ Wizard Whitebeard
- ☐ Odlaw

2. What color are the helpers' bow ties?
- ☐ Red
- ☐ Blue
- ☐ White

3. How many umbrellas are there?
- ☐ Three
- ☐ Four
- ☐ Five

4. What big thing are two waiters carrying?
- ☐ A bone
- ☐ A leash
- ☐ A pogo stick

5. What instrument is a waiter playing?
- ☐ Piano
- ☐ Accordion
- ☐ Guitar

6. What equipment can be found in the playground?
- ☐ Swings and a merry-go-round
- ☐ A seesaw and a slide
- ☐ Swings and a slide

EXTRA BONE-OCULAR EYE-BOGGLER

Study these close-ups carefully and turn back the page to find them.

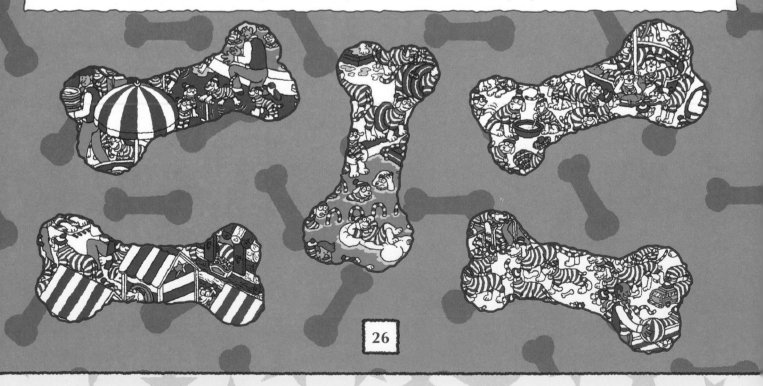

26

FIVE-MINUTE CHALLENGE Study the picture again, and write two extra questions to challenge a friend:
1: ....
2: ....

BULL'S-EYE!

Help Woof reach the target in the center of the maze by passing all five of his dog pals but avoiding the bulls. It's a-maze-ing!

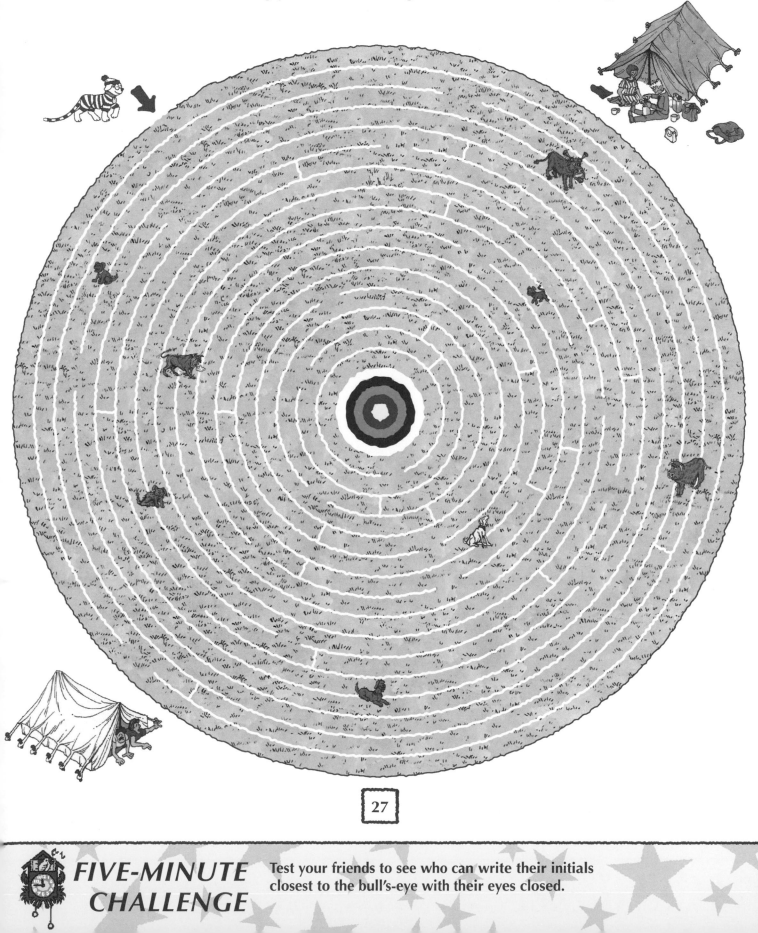

FIVE-MINUTE CHALLENGE

Test your friends to see who can write their initials closest to the bull's-eye with their eyes closed.

FLOWER POWER

Can you fill in the missing numbers? Each colored group of nine squares must contain the numbers 1–9, as must each row that goes up and down or left to right. You may prefer to write in pencil!

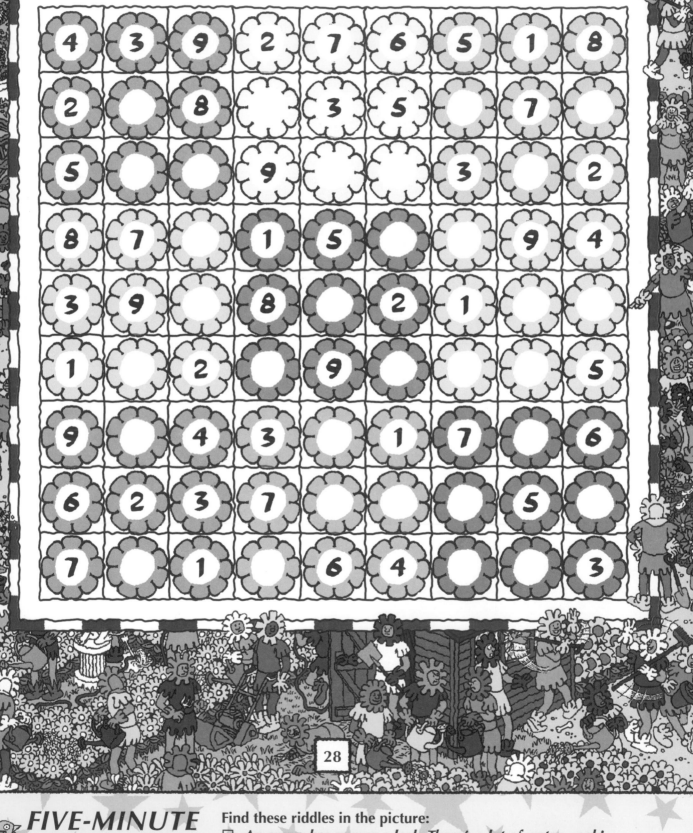

FIVE-MINUTE CHALLENGE

Find these riddles in the picture:
- ☐ *An arrow has sprung a leak. There's a lot of water—eek!*
- ☐ *A man on all fours, but without Woof-like paws!*

FRUIT PUNCH

Study the fruit in the puzzle closely—to the left and right, above and below. There are two zesty kinds of fruit that are always next to each other. Can you fill in the empty squares to keep them paired up?

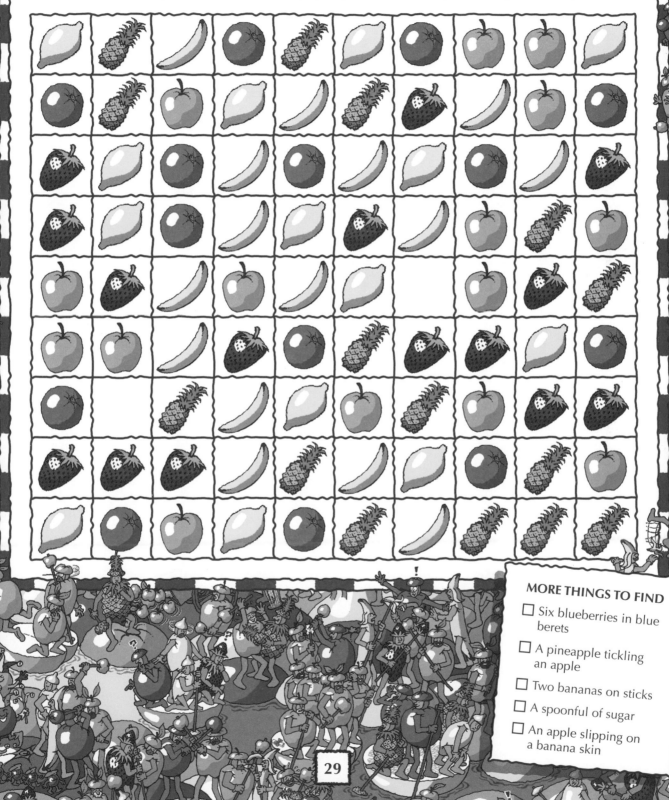

MORE THINGS TO FIND

☐ Six blueberries in blue berets

☐ A pineapple tickling an apple

☐ Two bananas on sticks

☐ A spoonful of sugar

☐ An apple slipping on a banana skin

29

FIVE-MINUTE CHALLENGE

Unscramble each of these words to discover two fruits you'd find in a smoothie!

- Sbtraawnbaenrary
- Ormaangnoge
- Ca$pheprrlye

BALLOON BINGO

Circle a number in the grid if you also see it on one of the ship balloons. Can you get five in a row?

1	7	18	6	12
25	19	2	15	21
10	3	17	22	5
14	8	11	23	16
9	20	24	13	4

30

MORE THINGS TO DO

✳ How did you win? Was it a line of vertical, horizontal, or diagonal numbers? Keep searching if you didn't get all three lines!

FIVE-MINUTE CHALLENGE

Using at least five numbers from the balloons, try to get to 346: you can add, divide, subtract, or multiply the numbers to get there!

NUMBER CRUNCHING

Solve the number puzzle to help Woof jump down through the clouds.
Subtract 1 from any red number and add 1 to any blue number.
Then draw a path to the finish by connecting the clouds that contain a sum of 5.

Start

Finish

31

MORE THINGS TO FIND

☐ A sailor with a blue beard
☐ Nine polka-dotted monsters
☐ The cloud with the highest final total

UP IN THE CLOUDS

Ta-da! Help Waldo hop to the finish by moving in repeated sequences of yellow, pink, white, and then blue clouds. He can only hop to a cloud that is next to the one he is on!

START

FINISH

32

FIVE-MINUTE CHALLENGE

Now, avoid landing on the pink clouds! You can go in any sequence, as long as you don't land on two same-colored clouds in a row.

BEHIND THE SCENES

Oh, no—Wenda's photographs printed out in funny colors!
Only two of these pictures are from the same scene—
can you work out which ones?

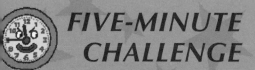

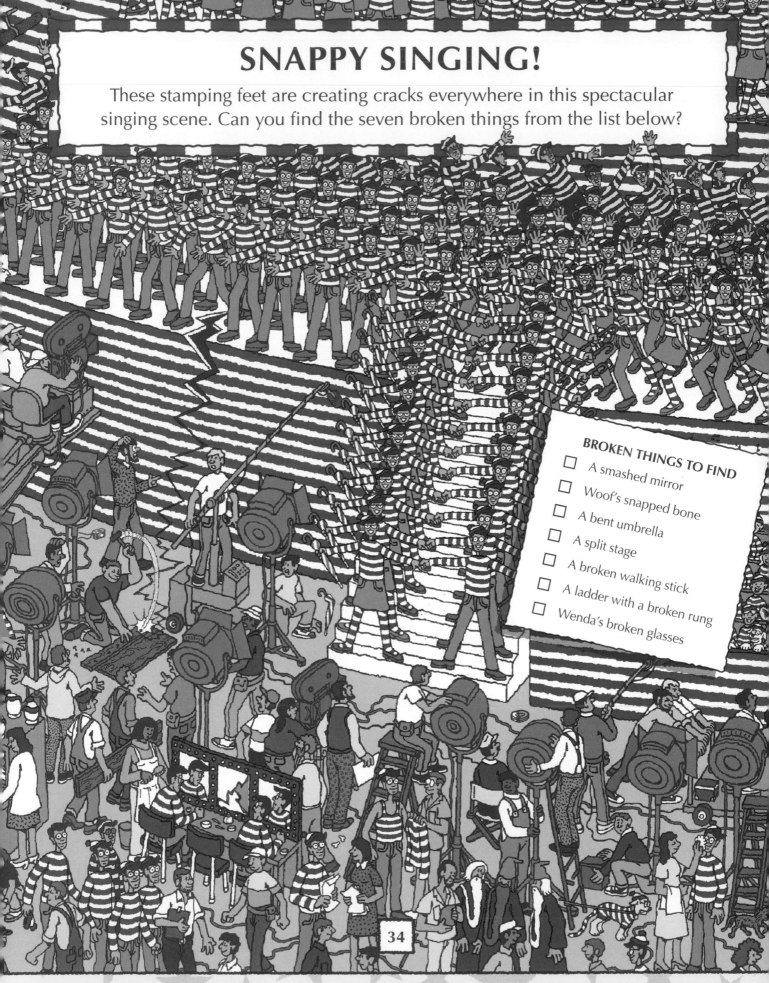

SNAPPY SINGING!

These stamping feet are creating cracks everywhere in this spectacular singing scene. Can you find the seven broken things from the list below?

BROKEN THINGS TO FIND
- ☐ A smashed mirror
- ☐ Woof's snapped bone
- ☐ A bent umbrella
- ☐ A split stage
- ☐ A broken walking stick
- ☐ A ladder with a broken rung
- ☐ Wenda's broken glasses

34

FIVE-MINUTE CHALLENGE

There's a lot of singing and dancing going on in this scene. Make up your very own funky dance move and write its name here!

MUSICAL FRAME FUN

Wenda has framed her favorite musical photographs. Can you find a picture that doesn't contain a musical note and one with Wenda's face in the frame?

MORE THINGS TO FIND
- [ ] Twelve violins
- [ ] A large bow tie
- [ ] A guitar
- [ ] Three tubas
- [ ] A one-eyed man

FIVE-MINUTE CHALLENGE

Find out who this famous artist is by using only this clue: In 1961, one of their paintings was accidentally hung upside down. It took forty-seven days for someone to notice!

WOBBLY WORD LADDERS

Hang on! Can you fill in the missing words in these ladders? Start at the top and work your way down by changing one letter at a time but keeping the rest of the letters in the same order.

HAT

MALT

_ _ _

_ _ _ _

_ _ _

_ _ _ _

KEY

_ _ _ _

GAME

MORE THINGS TO FIND

☐ A hat with a red pom-pom

☐ A parrot

☐ A football player

FIVE-MINUTE CHALLENGE

Try it again!
• In two steps, get from WOW to DOT
• In three steps, try SONG to FIND

TERRIFIC TITLES

FIVE-MINUTE CHALLENGE

Write in a title and author on the books above, then color in the covers.

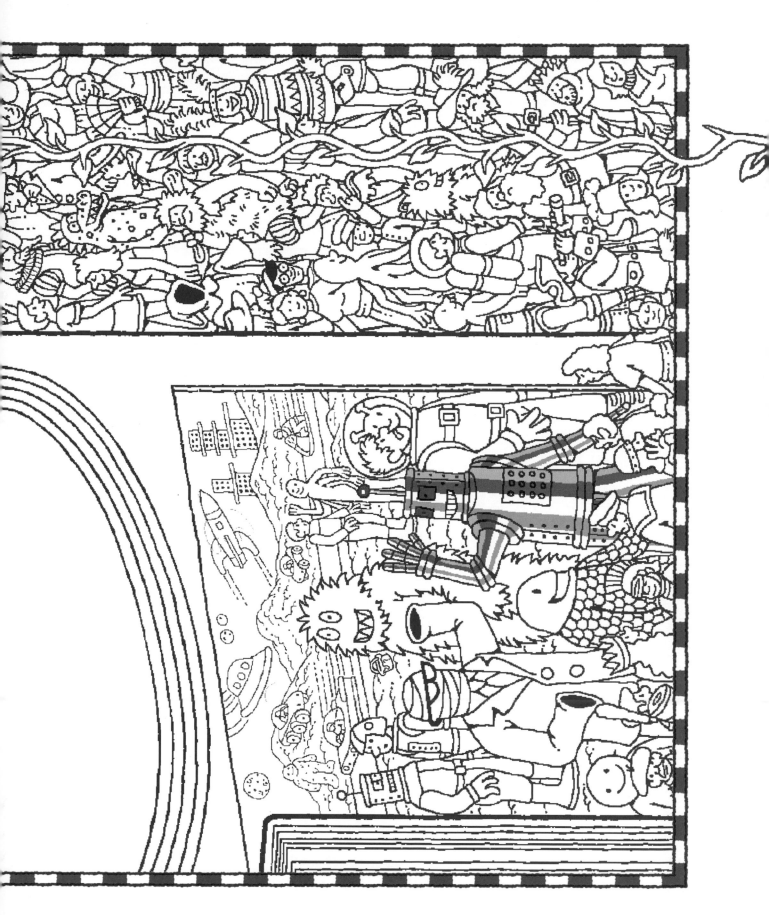

What a lot of literature! Color in these classic characters.

FIVE-MINUTE CHALLENGE

Guess the famous fairy tale from these three clues:

- I'm good at cleaning.
- I forgot to keep an eye on the time.
- I have unique feet.

TINSELTOWN

FIVE-MINUTE CHALLENGE

Unscramble these famous film characters and match them to their movie franchise!

- RATDH VARDE
- OB PEPE
- KEMIRT

- Star Wars
- Toy Story
- The Muppets

Lights, camera, action . . . color!

FIVE-MINUTE CHALLENGE

MORE THINGS TO FIND

☐ **An astronaut**
☐ **A rabbit**
☐ **A bendy telescope**

REELY FUN

Study the tiny pictures in the sprockets of the film reels, and find all the people and things (but not the stars) in the large pictures.

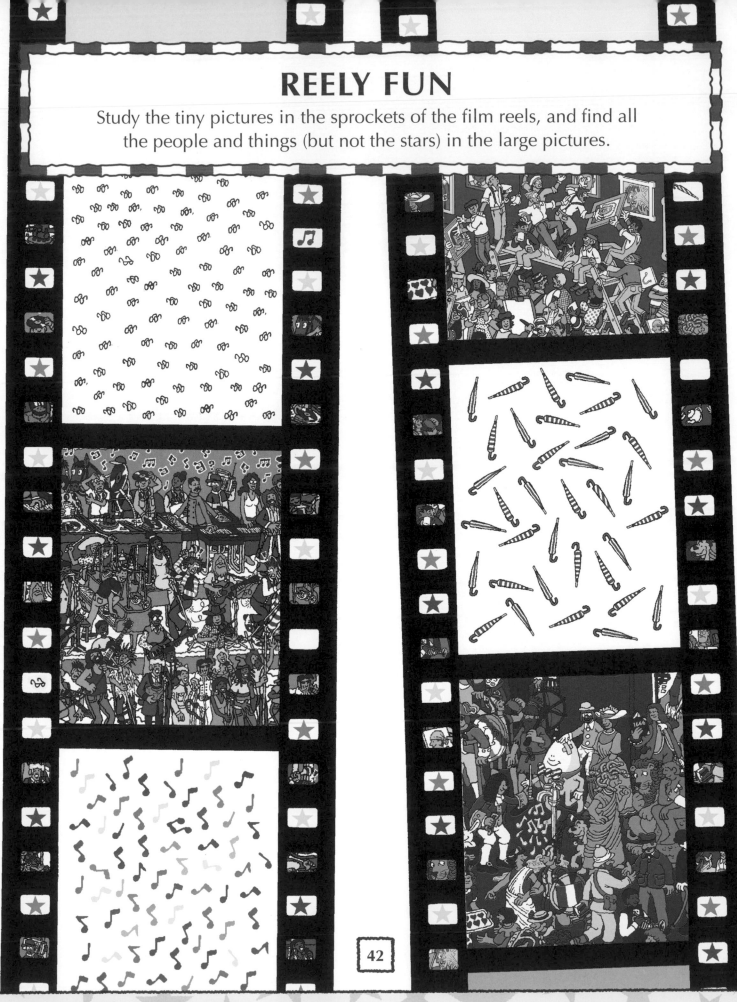

42

FIVE-MINUTE CHALLENGE

Look at the sequence of images shown in the sprockets of the film reels and fill in the two empty ones.

WHAT AN EXPRESSION!

Wenda here! My photos have come out funny!
Can you complete the unfinished portraits?
Then draw your own in the empty frames.

43

FIVE-MINUTE CHALLENGE

Find out the meaning of these fancy words for feelings:

- **Woebegone**
- **Beatific**
- **Splenetic**

CAMERA CLOSE-UPS

Whoops, Wenda's camera is broken! Can you figure out who she has accidentally zoomed in on? Some people appear more than once.

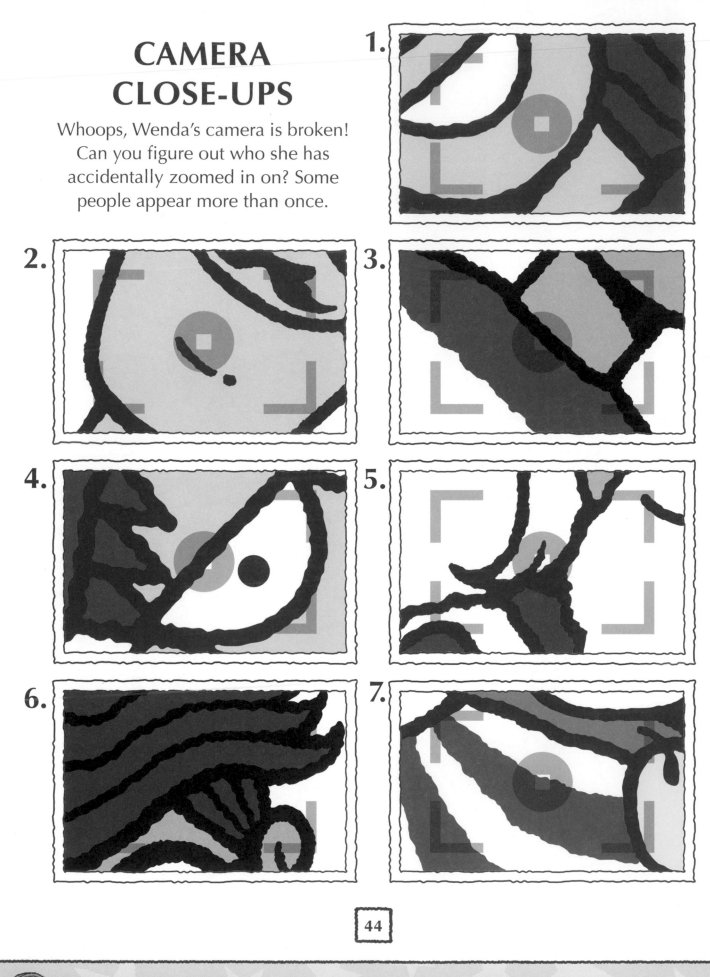

FACE IT

Yikes! This picture is mixed up. Guess who
it is and put it in the correct order by writing the numbers
1–6 in the boxes beside each strip.

45

FIVE-MINUTE CHALLENGE Find a famous face in a magazine that is large enough to cut into thick horizontal strips. Then mix it up for your friends to solve the puzzle.

SNAPSHOTS

Wenda loves taking pictures with her camera. Bring color to her photos and fill the blank spaces!

FIVE-MINUTE CHALLENGE

Put some filters on these photos! Try these effects on different snapshots:
• Only use the colors of the rainbow
• Make a striped or polka-dot pattern

FIVE-MINUTE CHALLENGE

Add snappy captions underneath the photos. They can just describe the scene, or you could add a joke or a piece of dialogue like a comic strip!

You have reached the end of
Waldo's vacation! Now look
back through the pages of his
journey and try to spot these things
that he saw along the way.

WALDO-CATION CHECKLIST

- [ ] A green hat with a red feather
- [ ] A singing cat
- [ ] A choking vine
- [ ] A periscope
- [ ] Cards playing cards
- [ ] A horse-drawn chariot
- [ ] A powder puff
- [ ] Two accordions
- [ ] Two cash registers
- [ ] Two knights
- [ ] A punctured hose
- [ ] Two witches in windows
- [ ] Two bull rings
- [ ] Two helicopters
- [ ] Three newspapers
- [ ] Someone dressed as a cake
- [ ] A topiary watering can
- [ ] A floating nose and mustache
- [ ] A red dress with white polka dots
- [ ] Seventeen magnifying glasses

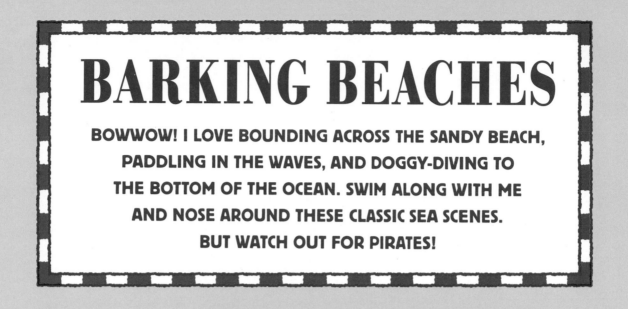

BARKING BEACHES

BOWWOW! I LOVE BOUNDING ACROSS THE SANDY BEACH,
PADDLING IN THE WAVES, AND DOGGY-DIVING TO
THE BOTTOM OF THE OCEAN. SWIM ALONG WITH ME
AND NOSE AROUND THESE CLASSIC SEA SCENES.
BUT WATCH OUT FOR PIRATES!

BARKING BOATS

Woof has gone to the seaside! Can you spot the sea-themed silhouettes in the scene below?

50

FIVE-MINUTE CHALLENGE

These ships don't have names! Choose some boats from the scene above and give them savvy seafaring titles!

Boat 1: ....

MORE THINGS TO FIND

☐ A Viking ship
☐ A lobster bed
☐ A cowboy riding a seahorse

Boat 2: ....
Boat 3: ....
Boat 4: ....
Boat 5: ....
Boat 6: ....

BOAT RACE DAY

Wow! What a wacky boat bonanza! There are six different races all happening at once. Can you match up the sets of flags to find out which boats are entered in which competition? There's Waldo's rowboat race, Woof's speedboat race, Wenda's build-your-own-raft race, Wizard Whitebeard's sailboat race, Odlaw's treasure hunt, and a who-can-catch-the-most-fish race.

Clue: Search for Waldo and his friends to find out which race is which!

52

MORE THINGS TO FIND

☐ A sea cowboy
☐ A mortarboard

SECRET SWIMATHON

Follow Waldo across the open waters until you find
the one boat with treasure stashed onboard.

❶ **First**, find a boat with a trail of steam that rises in and out of the water.
❷ **Jump overboard** and swim to a "school." Have a whale of a time!
❸ **Continue** on past a swordfight, to a man wearing a three-feathered
headdress. ❹ **"Duck" underwater** to something that is rubber and red
but not inflatable. ❺ **Swim behind** a "sea bed" to mermaids. Avoid the
tangled water-skiers! ❻ **Find** a bull and he will help you aboard!

53

- ☐ A pirate-y jack-in-the-box
- ☐ A flock of thieving seagulls
- ☐ A leaky diving suit
- ☐ A palm tree

WHAT A CATCH!

Odlaw's fishing for treasure.
Follow his line to find out what he's caught.

MORE THINGS TO FIND

☐ A fishing fish
☐ Two spotted fish
☐ A fish collision

54

FIVE-MINUTE CHALLENGE

There's a sea bed and a spyglass to catch, too! Draw in two other fishing vessels with tangly lines to these items, then challenge a friend to find out who caught what.

SEA SILHOUETTES

Study this busy beach scene to find each silhouette. Wow, what a sizzling search!

55

Unscramble these objects, then find them in the scene!

☐ Five SWOLET
☐ A CHABE ALBL
☐ Two MARECAS

MESSAGE IN A BOTTLE

Find seven real words or phrases by matching up
the pairs of papers. Write your answers in the bottle below.
You can use each piece more than once.

SURF

SUN

DECK

DIVE

CASE

SWIM

CAP

BOARD

SCUBA

BATHING

SUIT

CHAIR

1. ....
2. ....
3. ....
4. ....
5. ....
6. ....
7. ....

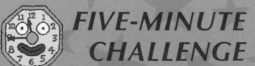

FIVE-MINUTE CHALLENGE

Four pairs of ripped edges fit perfectly together. Can you match
them all up? Which other beachy words can you make?

FISHING NET SETS

What a catch! Draw in the missing symbols. All nine must appear once in each box, but never in the same row.

FIVE-MINUTE CHALLENGE

Which of these fishy statements is false?

- Many fish have "gas bladders" that help them float.
- Sharks are the only fish with eyelids.
- Fish have no bones.

SEASHELLS GALORE

I see seashells on the seashore! Seek out and color in only the shells 🐚, not the pebbles ⬭, to reveal four items washed ashore.

MORE THINGS TO DO

✹ At the beach, collect flat stones (the size of a quarter). With a friend, take turns stacking one stone at a time. The winner is the one who doesn't topple the tower.

FIVE-MINUTE CHALLENGE

Solve these sea-deep riddles!

- What has a floor but no walls and waves without hands?
- What is the wettest letter in the alphabet?
- What do the letter *T* and an island have in common?

GONE FISHING

Who caught a jellyfish? Also, find one fish within each school of yellow, pink, blue, and green fish with different-colored fins.

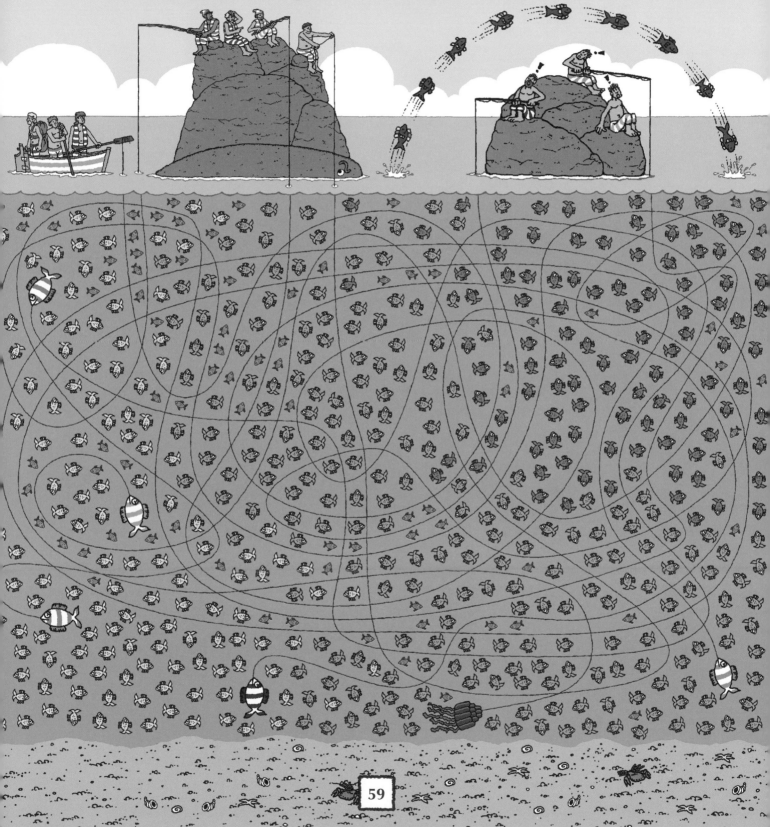

FIVE-MINUTE CHALLENGE

Pair up the striped fish to the stripes of five fishermen. What color fish is missing?

59

DEEP-SEA DIVE

Choose a start picture. Then move to any square that shares one identical creature (including color). The squares do not have to be touching. Keep going until you find a combination that gets you to a finish. Your moves will take you all over the place! You can go diagonally, down and up and down again, and jump however many rows you like.

FIVE-MINUTE
CHALLENGE

Play the game above again, but avoid different creatures each time:

- A can of sardines
- Turtles
- Jellyfish

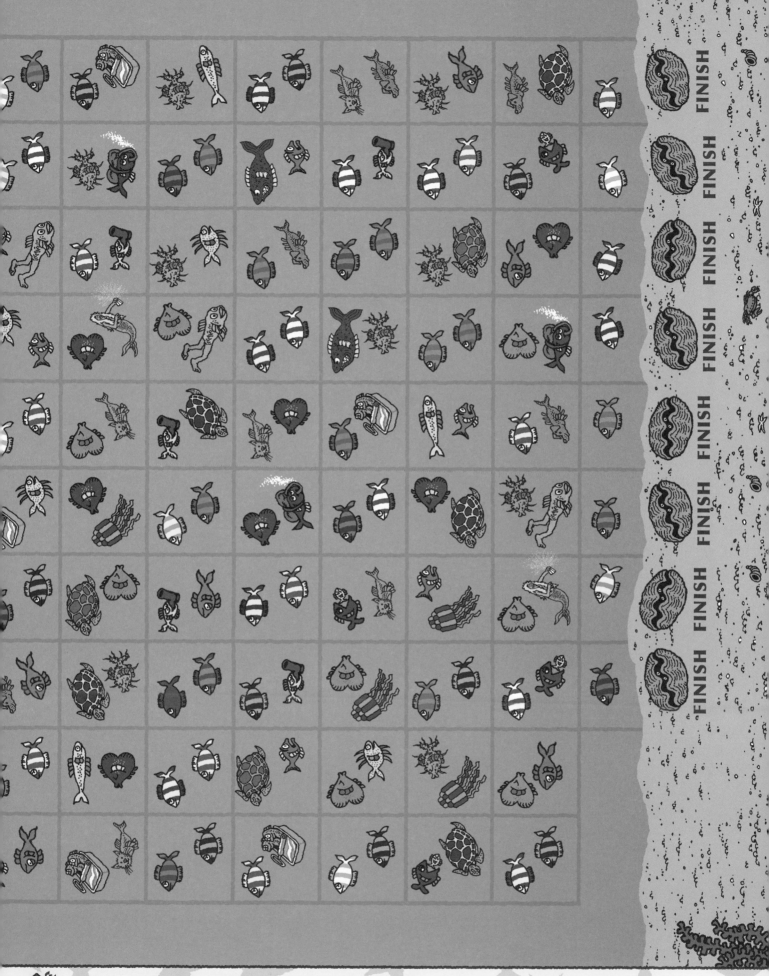

FINISH FINISH FINISH FINISH FINISH FINISH FINISH FINISH FINISH FINISH

FIVE-MINUTE CHALLENGE

Here's a tricky test! Can you find two squares in the game that are not possible to land on, no matter which route you take from the start?

BLOWING BUBBLES

Glug, glug! Cross out the three letters that spell the word *pop* in each bubble. Then unscramble the rest of the letters to spell eleven words.

62

MORE THINGS TO FIND
☐ A yellow starfish
☐ A bucket
☐ Woof's tail
☐ Five swimmers wearing green stripes

SEA SETS

Match each sea creature, scuba diver, and item under the sea with one or more identical copies to find an odd one out. It's maritime mayhem down there!

FIVE-MINUTE CHALLENGE

Can you spot these punny fish?

- ☐ Sea-lion
- ☐ Fish-cake
- ☐ Saw-fish

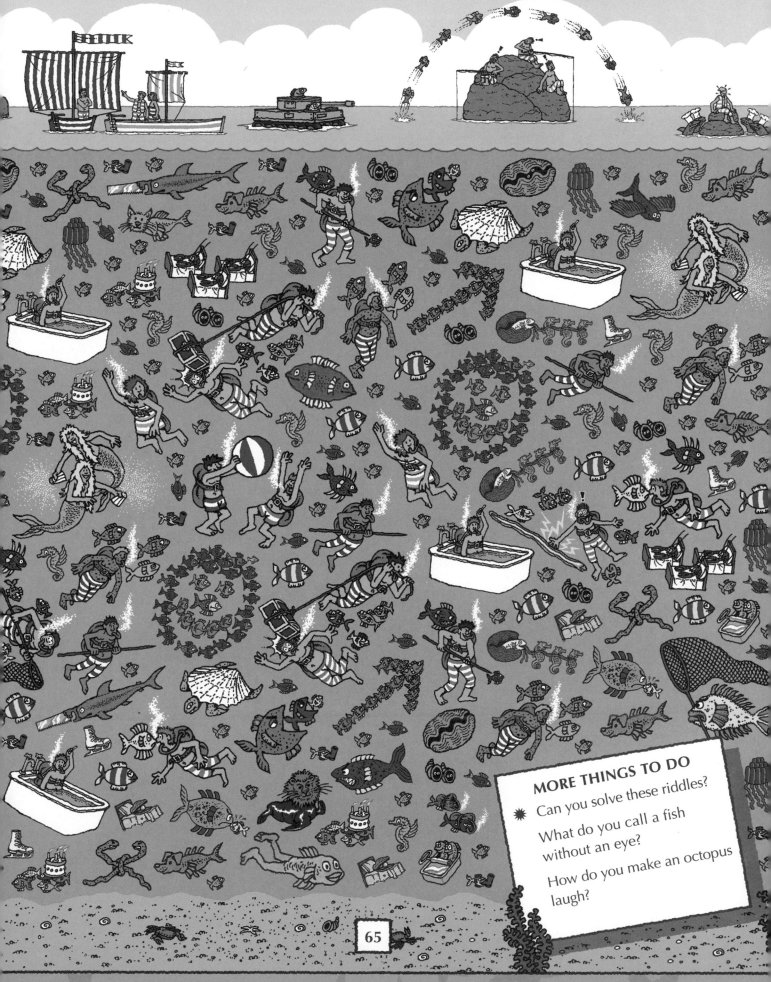

MORE THINGS TO DO

✳ Can you solve these riddles?

What do you call a fish without an eye?

How do you make an octopus laugh?

FIVE-MINUTE CHALLENGE

Draw and label your own funny fish creation!

SOMETHING FISHY

Match up the sets of three identically colored fish. One fish is not part of a set, so have a splish-splashing time finding out which one!

MORE THINGS TO FIND

- ☐ A smiling fish
- ☐ An angry fish
- ☐ A fish with closed eyes

66

FIVE-MINUTE CHALLENGE

Try saying this as many times as possible without tripping up on your words!

Fast flying fish have fantastic flapping fins.

SNAKY SEARCH

Find the *S* words in the word search below. Letters must run continuously, but they can go in any direction as long as the sides of their hexagons touch. Sssneaky!

Stripes
Slippery
Sea snake
Scaly skin
Spots
Snakebite

67

MORE THINGS TO FIND
☐ One repeated word that is backward
☐ A word that isn't a snake (but you might mistake it for one!)

MAKE A MONSTROSITY

Create your very own sea creature and color in the surrounding scene. What do you think is lurking at the bottom of this deep, dark sea? Eeek!

68

FIVE-MINUTE CHALLENGE Think up some accessories for your sea creature. You could draw a jaunty captain's hat, a hand (or fin!), a bag, a pair of goggles, maybe even its own pet!

SUPER-SNEAKY SEA-GAZING GAME

Odlaw loves to look out to sea with his pirate friends. Study the scene closely and find everything noted in the ship's logbook below.

- ☐ Three men wearing skull-and-crossbones T-shirts
- ☐ Two hats with green feathers
- ☐ Three men with yellow beards
- ☐ Four men wearing red-and-white-striped pants
- ☐ Three men wearing yellow bandanas with black spots
- ☐ Five flying swords

69

FIVE-MINUTE CHALLENGE

How many seafaring vessels are pictured in the scene above?

- Sixteen
- Ten
- Fourteen

SUPER-SNEAKY SEA-GAZING GAME

How closely did you study Odlaw's pirate scene? Look through these binocular views and find them on the previous page.

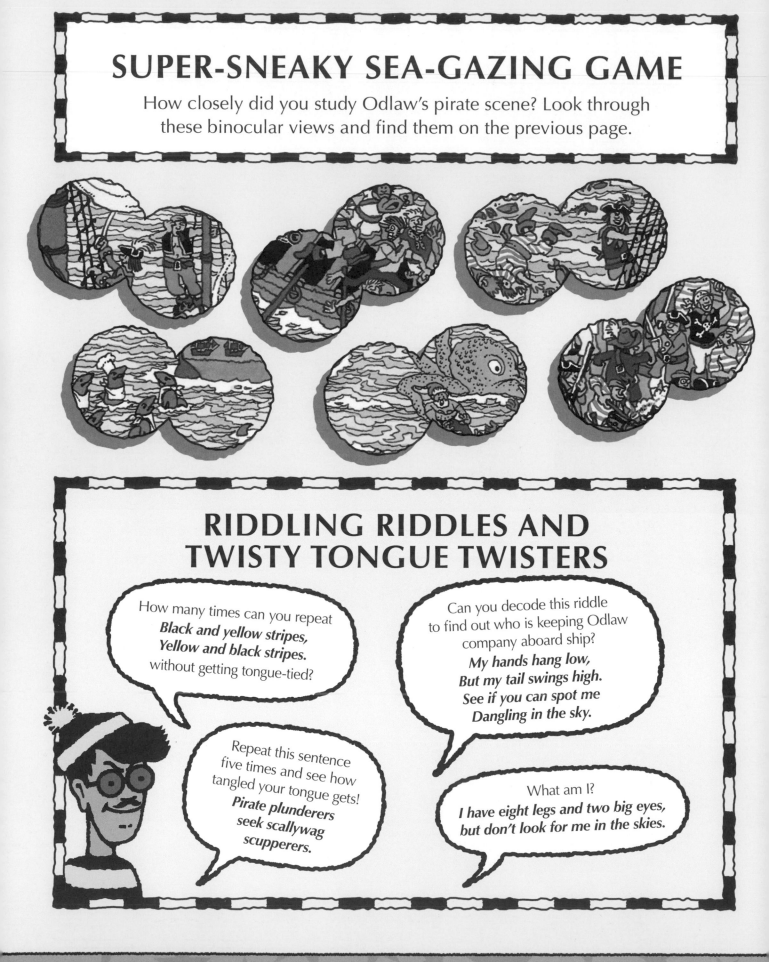

RIDDLING RIDDLES AND TWISTY TONGUE TWISTERS

How many times can you repeat
**Black and yellow stripes,
Yellow and black stripes.**
without getting tongue-tied?

Can you decode this riddle
to find out who is keeping Odlaw
company aboard ship?
**My hands hang low,
But my tail swings high.
See if you can spot me
Dangling in the sky.**

Repeat this sentence
five times and see how
tangled your tongue gets!
**Pirate plunderers
seek scallywag
scupperers.**

What am I?
**I have eight legs and two big eyes,
but don't look for me in the skies.**

FIVE-MINUTE CHALLENGE

Turn back the page and choose two more fiendish things to find, then challenge a friend to search for them.

1. ....
2. ....

I-SPY-RATE

Color in these pesky pirates.

71

FIVE-MINUTE CHALLENGE

Color in these pieces as quickly as you can. Y'arrrgh!

• Every hat
• All the treasure
• Waldo

COLORING CAVE

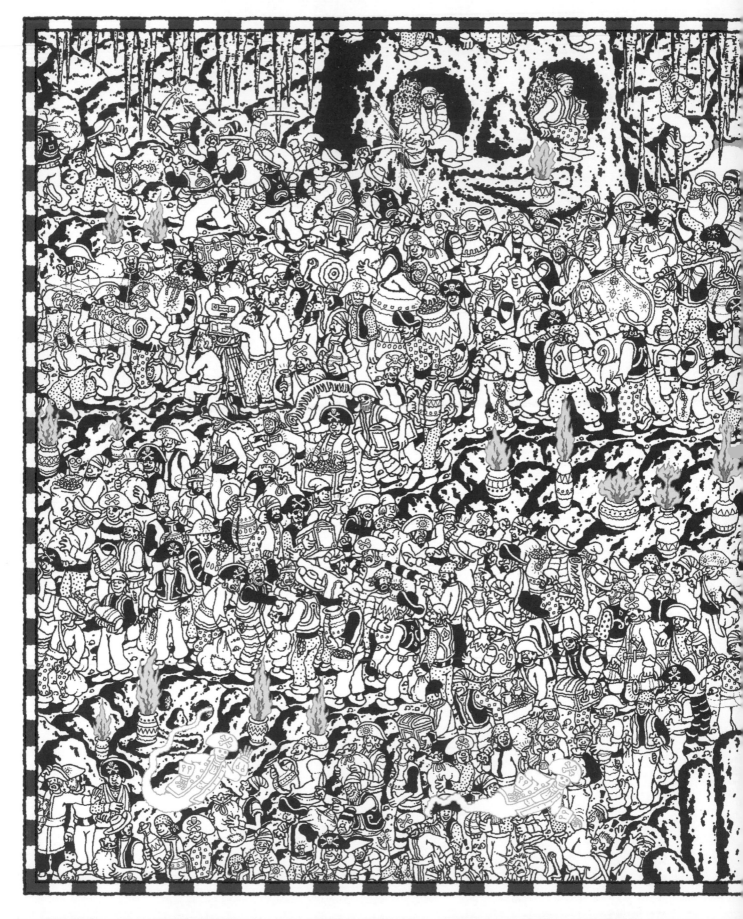

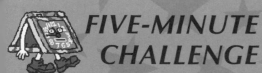

FIVE-MINUTE CHALLENGE

Searches ahoy! Seek out and color in these pirate-y sights:

Add some magic sparkle to this shiny treasure trove!
And shiver me timbers! Search for three pirate ghosts!

- ☐ A maiden on a throne
- ☐ Someone sleeping
- ☐ Miners
- ☐ A startled horse
- ☐ A kennel
- ☐ A clapper board
- ☐ A literal chest of drawers

PATH OF THE PLUNDERING PIRATES

Can you navigate your way around the ship, then reach the desert islands?

❶ **Start** by the man in yellow pants standing on one leg. Walk along the mast pole, but beware of the cannonballs! ❷ **Climb down** the shroud net without bumping into the brawling shipmates. ❸ **Hop along** the deck and say hello to Woof (all you can see is his tail!), then follow the pirate with a cutlass in his mouth up to the first crow's nest.

FIVE-MINUTE CHALLENGE   **Find out the meaning of these classic pirate phrases:**

❹ **Take a right** along the middle mast and climb the rope to the top. ❺ **Leap onto** the mast of the skull-and-crossbones boat. ❻ **Swerve around** the three pirates gawking at Tarzan. ❼ **Head toward** the swinging gorilla, then zip-line down past the collapsing sail to the bowsprit. ❽ **Slide down** toward the drinking pirates, then shuffle to the very edge. ❾ **Time to** take the plunge! Call a mighty "Y'ARGHHH!" then dive into the deep blue sea and swim toward the desert islands.

- Ahoy!
- Aye aye
- Blimey
- Dungbie
- Grub
- Hornswaggler
- Me hearties
- Pieces of eight
- Sea dog
- Shanty

PIRATE-Y PUZZLE

Avast, me hearties! What a puzzling picture! Can you find the correct three missing pieces? Arrr!

FIVE-MINUTE CHALLENGE

Study the picture and each puzzle piece carefully. How many of these can you find?

.... pirates wearing stripes
.... skull-and-crossbones
.... cannons

SKULL AND CROSSWORD

Ahoy there! Fill in the answers next to these questions to reveal a word going downward that is Odlaw's favorite part of a pirate-y disguise!

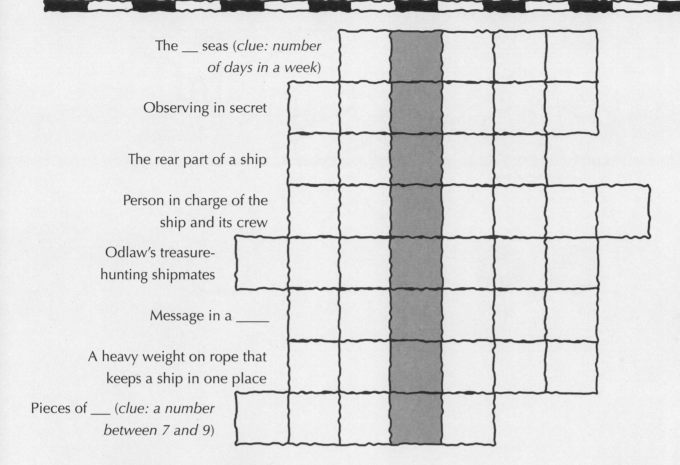

The __ seas (*clue: number of days in a week*)

Observing in secret

The rear part of a ship

Person in charge of the ship and its crew

Odlaw's treasure-hunting shipmates

Message in a ____

A heavy weight on rope that keeps a ship in one place

Pieces of __ (*clue: a number between 7 and 9*)

77

FIVE-MINUTE CHALLENGE

Make your own pirate spyglass. Roll a piece of paper into a tube and decorate it. What can you see?

SKULDUGGERY

Odlaw has mixed up the skull-and-crossbones flag!
Can you draw it in the right order in the grid below?

MORE THINGS TO DO

Create your own pirate name by choosing:

Your favorite color: ....
A body part or animal: ....
Your last name: ....

FIVE-MINUTE CHALLENGE

Now ask your friends and family to create their own pirate names, to gather a mighty pirate crew!

PIECES OF EIGHT

Look closely at the pictures in the coins to find out which ones are in the scene. Be warned, four of them are from elsewhere in the book! Yo, ho, ho!

MORE THINGS TO DO

❋ Being a pirate is all about luck! Toss a coin: heads, you're a pirate; tails, you're a fisherman!

FIVE-MINUTE CHALLENGE

Take the Xs out of these words to reveal locations on a treasure map!

BXLAXCXKBXEXARXD BXAAXXYX
CXRXOCOXDIXLXE XCOXVEX
LOXNXG JXOHXNX LXAAXXKXEX

FIVE-MINUTE CHALLENGE

Color in all the hats and bushy beards, using a different color or pattern for each one!

PICTURE–PIRATE

It's time to get even more creative and fill these frames with art of your own!

FIVE-MINUTE CHALLENGE

MORE THINGS TO FIND

☐ Two musical notes
☐ A mysterious paint pot
☐ Two berets

Woof *shore* had a great adventure! Bound back through the pages of his walkabout and help him sniff out these things on the way.

BARKING BEACHES CHECKLIST

- [ ] Seasick sailors
- [ ] A pair of dice
- [ ] Five pirate ghosts
- [ ] An angry shield
- [ ] A T-shirt with a green pocket
- [ ] A furry coat
- [ ] Flying fish
- [ ] A fake shark fin
- [ ] A crab on someone's head
- [ ] A hand made of stone
- [ ] Three pool floats
- [ ] A fish bowl
- [ ] A winking skull-and-crossbones
- [ ] Waldo on a desert island
- [ ] Underwater deck chairs
- [ ] A fanged beast stuck in an ax
- [ ] Two skull-and-crossbone coins
- [ ] A crow wearing a pirate's hat
- [ ] Someone standing on an octopus
- [ ] Someone "walking the plank"

TIME TO BUILD A MACHINE

Design your own time machine in the space below.

FIVE-MINUTE CHALLENGE

Your machine needs an instruction manual. Don't forget to label everything to show how it works!

TICK-TOCK MEMORY GAME

You have two minutes to study all the doors in the picture and the keys above them. Then turn the page to test your memory!

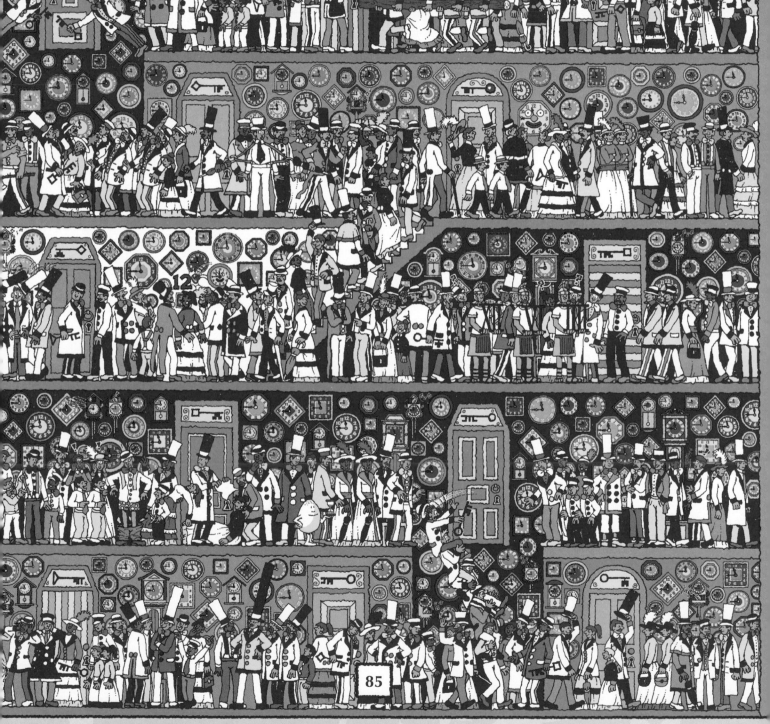

FIVE-MINUTE CHALLENGE

After you test your memory, try looking for:

- ☐ An egg timer
- ☐ Ten cuckoo clocks
- ☐ Roman numerals

TICK-TOCK MEMORY GAME

Can you remember which key goes above which door?
Draw a line from each key to the door it opens.

THROUGH THE KEYHOLE GAME

Take your time peeking through these keyholes.
Then turn back the page and find each section in the scene.

86

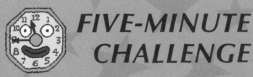

FIVE-MINUTE CHALLENGE

Study the picture again and write down three extra things to find. Then challenge a friend!

1. ....
2. ....
3. ....

TIME VORTEX

Going back in time can make things a bit strange! Color in as much as you can, but avoid using everyone's usual colors (e.g., no red on Waldo!).

87

FIVE-MINUTE CHALLENGE

Would you rather travel back in time or into the future? Make a pros-and-cons list for both with your friends!

GREAT GUIDEBOOKS

Off we go! Cross out ten books that the riddles
rule out to reveal the one I'm taking on my travels.

The book you're looking for:

* Has no shields or swords . . .

* or anything made of bricks or stone.

* It's not about four-legged creatures.

* No cameras are allowed.

* Its travel tips go beyond the globe.

* It's full of mysteries, but they are
  not golden.

* Its route may (or may not!) take you
  north, south, east, or west.

Animal Antics

STONE AGE ART

HOW TO TAME A MONSTER

The Secrets of Ancient Gold

THE LAST DAYS OF THE AZTECS

TRAVELING THE WORLD

ANCIENT ROME

THE RIDDLE OF THE PYRAMIDS

WENDA'S PHOTOGRAPHY GUIDE

At the Castle

ODLAW'S SNEAKY DIRECTIONS

MORE THINGS TO DO

* Keep your eyes
  peeled for lands
  on Wenda's
  route where
  some of these
  great guidebooks
  might be useful.

88

FIVE-MINUTE CHALLENGE

Each of the characters and objects on these
covers appears somewhere else in this book.
How many can you find in five minutes?

PLAY BALL

Can you work out which rocks come next in these four sequences?

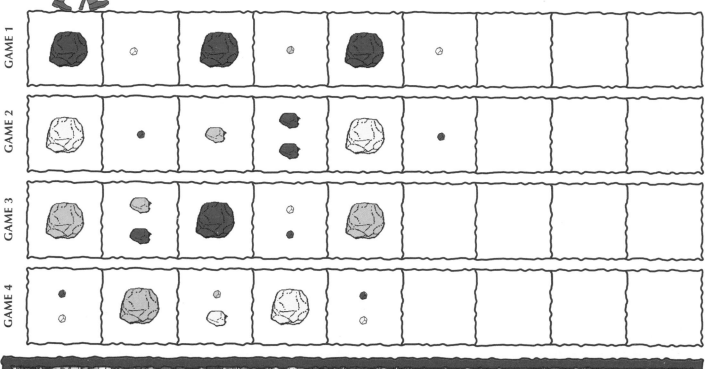

GAME 1

GAME 2

GAME 3

GAME 4

MORE THINGS TO FIND

☐ Ten blue-and-white-striped dinosaurs

☐ A dinosaur with a blue horn

☐ Two red dinosaurs hiding under a pink dinosaur

FIVE-MINUTE CHALLENGE

Create your own sequence of rocks. First draw the outlines, then color them in!

DINO-RAMA

 FIVE-MINUTE CHALLENGE Fill the white border with doodles of dinosaur bones! How many can you draw in five minutes?

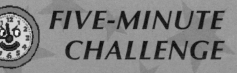

FIVE-MINUTE CHALLENGE

Disentangle these dino names, then find them and color them in the scene:

- CRITATOPSER ....
- TEDOPRACTLY ....
- OSCUDIPLOD ....

TRUTH OR TAILS?

Test your knowledge of Woof's ancient four-legged friends and work out which statements are true and which are false.

1. The word dinosaur means "terrible lizard."

2. A dinosaur scientist is called a dinotologist.

3. Dinosaurs laid eggs.

4. This anagram spells a dinosaur's name: RETTSRIPOCA

5. A tyrannosaurus's bite was roughly three times stronger than that of a lion.

6. The ankylosaurus had a club tail.

7. The dinosaur with the longest name is a micropachycephalosaurus.

8. A pterodactyl had three wings.

9. A brachiosaurus had a very short neck.

10. The dinosaurs lived until sixty-five thousand years ago.

Use the Internet or an encyclopedia to look up more fun facts about dinosaurs!

DID YOU KNOW?

There was a dinosaur similar to a dog! It is called Cynognathus (*sy-nog-nay-thus*) and was a hairy mammal-like animal with dog-like teeth. Woof claims that his great-great-great-grandfather was one (calculated in dog years, of course)!

ONE MORE THING!

What is the name of the dinosaur whose skeleton is in this picture? *Clue: it begins with the letter S.*

FIVE-MINUTE CHALLENGE

Find one true fact about dinosaurs and make up one false one, then challenge a friend to guess which is which!

WOOF'S WORD WHEEL

Use the clues to help you find five words using three or more letters in the word wheel. Each answer must contain the letter O only once.

CLUES

1. It's as hard as rock.
2. Woof's favorite thing
3. Used to sniff
4. Heads, shoulders, knees, and . . .
5. Woof is one of these.

2.

3.

4.

1.

5.

93

FIVE-MINUTE CHALLENGE   See how many other words you can make using the word wheel!

WOOF-A-SAURUS

FIVE-MINUTE CHALLENGE

Add dinosaurs to Woof's two unfinished dog tags.
BowWOW! Roar!

FIVE-MINUTE CHALLENGE

What do you call a dinosaur at the rodeo? A bronco-saurus! Ha, ha!

Once you've stopped chuckling, color in: • Every bone • Every scale • Every tooth!

SURVIVAL SEQUENCES

Study the order of the pictures in the example, then fill in the blanks in games 1, 2, and 3. (The sequence starts over again when it reaches the end symbol.)

FIVE-MINUTE CHALLENGE   Draw your own stick-figure sequence!

CAVE LIFE QUIZ

We stumbled upon amazing caves! Here are questions to bamboozle your brain. Some have more than one answer!

1. The Stone Age is called the Stone Age because:
- ☐ tools were made of stone
- ☐ beds were made of rocks
- ☐ dinosaurs threw stones

2. During this time, the people:
- ☐ hunted and gathered food
- ☐ didn't hunt for food
- ☐ got takeout

3. Found on cave walls were:
- ☐ paintings of animals
- ☐ magic doors
- ☐ paintings of dragons

4. Found in caves were:
- ☐ bears
- ☐ baboons
- ☐ lions

5. Mastodons looked like:
- ☐ elephants
- ☐ mice
- ☐ dogs

6. These things were woolly:
- ☐ rhinos
- ☐ mammoths
- ☐ fish

7. Cave dwellers knew how to make:
- ☐ fire
- ☐ origami
- ☐ lasagna

8. Wild boars are most closely related to:
- ☐ platypuses
- ☐ porcupines
- ☐ pigs

9. Animal skins and bones were used to make:
- ☐ clothes
- ☐ tools
- ☐ dish detergent

10. Handmade tools included:
- ☐ shields
- ☐ spears
- ☐ swords

97

FIVE-MINUTE CHALLENGE

MORE THINGS TO FIND
- ☐ Two cave bears
- ☐ A stone wheel
- ☐ A washing line
- ☐ Two red apples
- ☐ Ten cave dogs

WRITE LIKE AN EGYPTIAN

Decode the ancient message using the scroll of hieroglyphics.

FIVE-MINUTE CHALLENGE

Use the blank scroll above to write your name in hieroglyphics.

PYRAMID PUZZLE

Search for the words at the bottom of this page in the pyramid puzzle.
The words go up, down, forward, and backward.

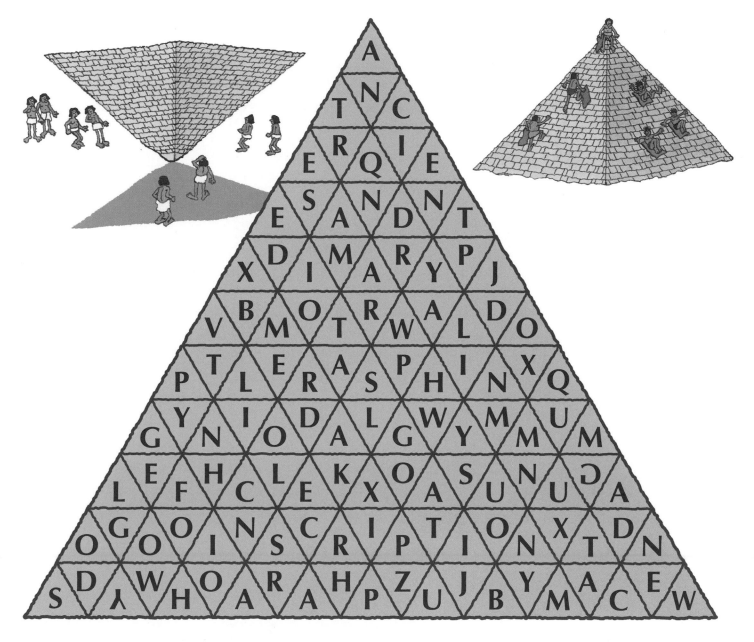

ANCIENT • CAT • DESERT • EGYPT
GOAT • GODS • INSCRIPTION • MUMMY
NILE • PHARAOH • PYRAMID • SAND
SPHINX • SUN • TOMB • WALDO

99

FIVE-MINUTE CHALLENGE

MORE THINGS TO FIND

☐ A backward letter
☐ An upside-down letter
☐ The names of two of Waldo's friends

IMAGINE YOUR CITY!

Use the triangles as a guide to build and color in your very own Egyptian city.

FIVE-MINUTE CHALLENGE

The Ancient Egyptians used to worship cats as gods, so add a pharaoh-worthy cat to your Egyptian city!

VERUM AUT FALSUM?

We've roamed all the way back to ancient Rome!
Test your knowledge and work out whether
these statements are true or false:

I. THE ROMAN EMPIRE WAS THE LARGEST EMPIRE IN HISTORY.

II. NEMESIS WAS THE ROMAN GODDESS OF REVENGE.

III. SACRED GEESE SAVED ROME IN 390 BCE.

IV. JULIUS CAESAR WAS AN EMPEROR.

V. ACCORDING TO LEGEND, THE FOUNDERS OF ROME WERE RAISED BY A WOLF.

VI. THE ROMANS WORE TOGAS EVERY DAY.

VII. CONCRETE WAS INVENTED BY THE ROMANS.

VIII. PLUTO WAS THE ROMAN GOD OF THE UNDERWORLD.

IX. DORMICE WERE A DELICACY SERVED AT BANQUETS.

X. ONLY MEN COULD BE GLADIATORS.

FIVE-MINUTE CHALLENGE

MORE THINGS TO FIND

☐ A sad lion
☐ An emperor assassin
☐ Twenty-two red shields

SPECTATOR SPORT

Match each person and object in the central, sandy arena with one or more identical copies to reveal the odd one out.

FIVE-MINUTE CHALLENGE

Ancient Romans had lots of different gods and goddesses. Can you match the name to what they were in charge of?

MORE THINGS TO DO

* Draw sandals on some of the Romans' bare feet!

* Think up tricks for taming lions, leopards, and tigers.

JUPITER   VENUS   MINERVA   MARS   MERCURY   DIANA   NEPTUNE

Travel   Thunder   Seas   Hunting   Wisdom   Love   War

BUILDING BLOCKS

It's crazy and cryptic construction time! Can you complete each grid using only the shaped blocks shown underneath it?

HINT: If you get stuck, copy the pieces onto grid paper and cut them out to try different combinations until you get it right!

FIVE-MINUTE CHALLENGE

Try drawing different-size grids and filling them with some of the shapes above. You can make up your own combinations, too!

GAME, SET, AND MATCH

Can you copy these masks in the empty squares below them?

MORE THINGS TO FIND

☐ Two exhausted ball players

☐ Five red feathers in headbands

☐ A person wearing a red nose

☐ A man wearing clown shoes

105

FIVE-MINUTE CHALLENGE

Draw your very own masks in the two blank spaces above!

THE TERRIFIC TEMPLE TREK

Can you find the secret hiding place of the Aztec gold hoard? Follow the directions below.

❶ **Start your journey** by finding a Spanish conquistador holding a flag with a double-headed eagle on it. ❷ **Walk along** the base of the pyramid and climb up the tower of soldiers until you reach the man with the very tall red-and-orange feather headdress. Be careful not to get hit on the head! ❸ **Climb over** to the stairs at his right and run up to the platform at the top. Greet the man with the staff.

FIVE-MINUTE CHALLENGE

MORE THINGS TO FIND
- ☐ Nine birds
- ☐ Thirty shields with feathers

- ☐ A man covering his ears
- ☐ Three men wearing gold medallions

❹ **Slide down** the right-hand side of the stairs. Once you get past the falling rock, see if you can find the man with closed eyes holding a crossbow in one hand. ❺ **At ground level** walk to the right and find an Aztec warrior holding a yellow-and-black-striped shield (do you think he knows Odlaw?). ❻ **Crawl over** to another dropped yellow-and-black-striped shield. Avoid the falling man! ❼ **Jump onto** the gray horse and let the helmeted rider trot you around the corner. ❽ **Tiptoe up** the stairs to the top. ❾ **Dash into** the open mouth without being seen!

☐ A pickpocket
☐ Eleven men in yellow costumes with black spots

Which is not true about Aztecs?
• They introduced chocolate to Europe.
• They lived in the jungle.

• They were originally known as Mexicas. Europeans invented the word *Aztec*.

NORSE CODE

Decode the second message to help you find a treasure map on this page. Start by copying over any letters with the same Norse letter, then fill in the blanks.

MESSAGE ONE

	V	I	K	I	N	G	S		A	R	E

O	D	L	A	W	S		F	R	I	E	N	D	S

MESSAGE TWO

FIVE-MINUTE CHALLENGE

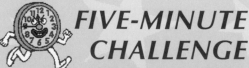

There's time for one more message, and it comes with a challenge: decode it as quickly as you can!

FUNNY FACE FLAGS

What a frenzied flurry of fierce and funny flags! Can you find these eleven foolish faces in the scene below?

109

MORE THINGS TO FIND

☐ Two snakes
☐ A game of tic-tac-toe
☐ Ten milk bottles

MEDIEVAL MAGIC

We've gone all the way back to the Middle Ages! See if you can spot these colorful characters in the scene:

FIVE-MINUTE CHALLENGE

Animals could be tried and convicted for crimes in the Middle Ages! Invent your own criminal creature following the example here:

MORE THINGS TO FIND

- [ ] An apple thief
- [ ] A juggling jester
- [ ] A band of minstrels
- [ ] An angry fish

Name: Rodney the Rude
Crime: Throwing carrots at children
Punishment: Eating moldy lettuce

Name: ....
Crime: ....
Punishment: ....

FLIP FLOP
SILHOUETTES

Sit opposite a friend and see who can be first to match the silhouettes to the scene!

A B C D E

FIVE-MINUTE CHALLENGE

MORE THINGS TO FIND
- ☐ A knight
- ☐ A teapot
- ☐ Three dogs
- ☐ A kangaroo
- ☐ A wheelbarrow

FIVE-MINUTE CHALLENGE

MORE THINGS TO FIND
- ☐ A motorbike
- ☐ A mallet
- ☐ Two blue feathers
- ☐ An astronaut
- ☐ A bandage

COUNT OF THE CASTLE

Free the five prisoners locked in the castle tower, then race to the finish! A great game for one (or more) players.

FIVE-MINUTE CHALLENGE

Try the game again with this extra challenge: if you land on a magic door, you have to start over! How far can you get in five minutes?

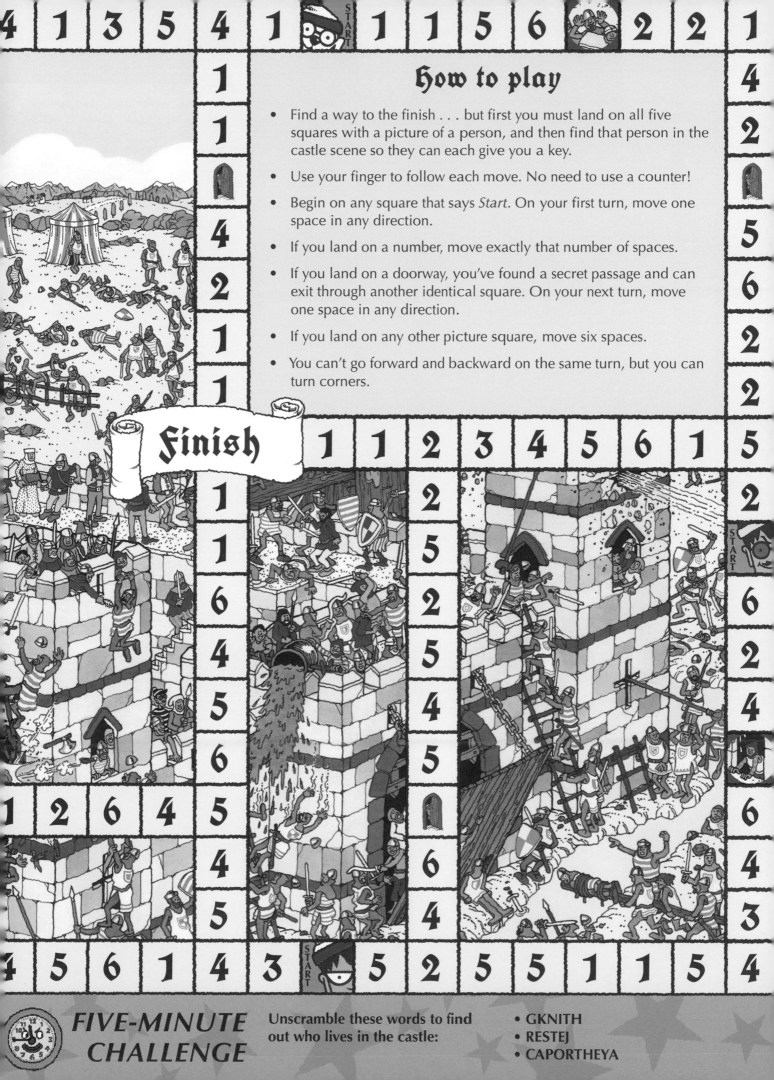

How to play

- Find a way to the finish . . . but first you must land on all five squares with a picture of a person, and then find that person in the castle scene so they can each give you a key.

- Use your finger to follow each move. No need to use a counter!

- Begin on any square that says *Start*. On your first turn, move one space in any direction.

- If you land on a number, move exactly that number of spaces.

- If you land on a doorway, you've found a secret passage and can exit through another identical square. On your next turn, move one space in any direction.

- If you land on any other picture square, move six spaces.

- You can't go forward and backward on the same turn, but you can turn corners.

Finish

FIVE-MINUTE CHALLENGE

Unscramble these words to find out who lives in the castle:

- GKNITH
- RESTEJ
- CAPORTHEYA

WORD CASTLE

Find the words at the bottom of this page in the three-letter bricks
of this castle. A word can read across more than one brick.

R O F		A Q U	E E N		A O E
M X A		J O P	W W O		W G R
L W A	D R A	W B R	I D G	E H L	D R A
O A R	M O R	U E K	R C A	T A P	U L T
N T P	C A S	T L E	L Q P	U F M	P X E
W Q L	E U H	E L M	E T A	B A T	T L E
M O A	T H Y	K W S	E M I	U L E	I A F
D G E	M I L	A I N	S I S	W O R	D W R
A R R	O W H	R E E	A K L	K C E	T L H
H F M	A R A	W N P	M T L	H F L	A G T
W K I	N G O	H Y O	E A B	C R O	W N G

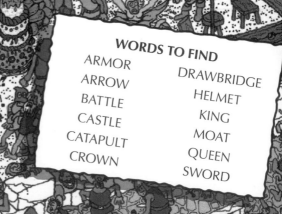

WORDS TO FIND

ARMOR
ARROW
BATTLE
CASTLE
CATAPULT
CROWN

DRAWBRIDGE
HELMET
KING
MOAT
QUEEN
SWORD

FIVE-MINUTE CHALLENGE

Work out the two magic words that can open the castle
drawbridge. Then find them hidden in the word castle!
Hint: The letters go up, across, and down. O _ _ _ / _ _ S _ _ E

SWASHBUCKLING CHAOS

Can you complete this jigsaw puzzle? Watch out: there's an extra piece!
(You can photocopy the page and cut out the pieces if you like.)

BURIED BONES

Woof has been busy burying bones! Can you fill in
the grid coordinates for the items at the bottom of
the page to mark where he has hidden them?

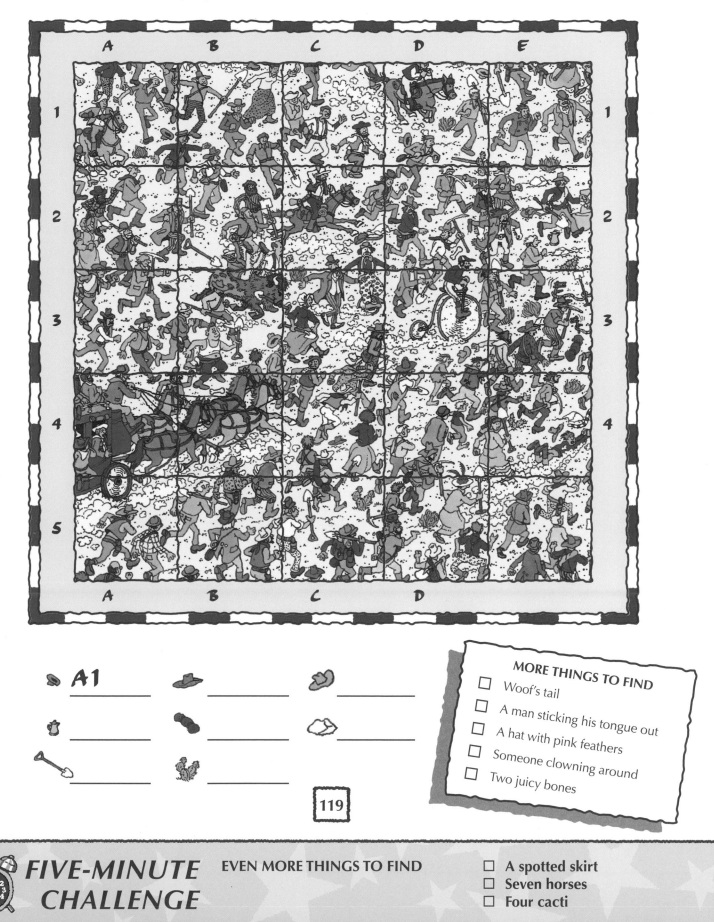

 A1 _____   _____   _____

_____   _____   _____

_____

MORE THINGS TO FIND
- ☐ Woof's tail
- ☐ A man sticking his tongue out
- ☐ A hat with pink feathers
- ☐ Someone clowning around
- ☐ Two juicy bones

FIVE-MINUTE CHALLENGE

EVEN MORE THINGS TO FIND
- ☐ A spotted skirt
- ☐ Seven horses
- ☐ Four cacti

COWBOY COLORS

Well, howdy, partner! Put down your pistols and pick up your pencils: it's colorin' time. Yee-haw!

SALOON

120

FIVE-MINUTE CHALLENGE

Color in all of:

☐ The cowboy hats
☐ The boots
☐ The wagon wheels

121

The townsfolk don't know which store is which! Can you write in the store names for them? Make sure they are fit for a gold-rush town!

DIGGING FOR GOLD

Yee-haw! The answers to this crossword puzzle are set in the Wild, Wild West.

Across

1. A large farm used to keep animals (5 letters)

3. The seat placed on a horse's back (6 letters)

4. A vessel with a handle used to carry water (6 letters)

6. Someone who works with iron and makes horseshoes (10 letters)

9. The opposite of cold (3 letters)

10. A tool used to dig: pick-__ (3 letters)

11. Midday (4 letters)

Down

1. To steal (3 letters)

2. Money offered on a poster for a wanted person (6 letters)

3. A rush of startled animals (8 letters)

5. A green plant with spikes (6 letters)

7. A looped rope used to catch horses (5 letters)

8. A form of transportation on rails (5 letters)

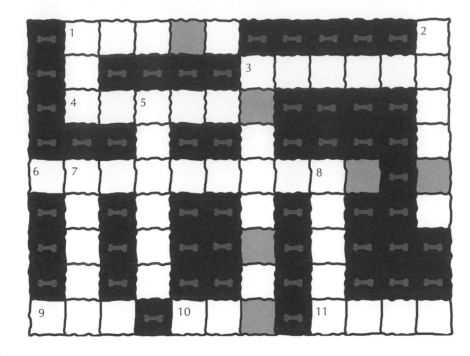

122

FIVE-MINUTE CHALLENGE

Unscramble the six letters in gray squares to spell out grid coordinates. Look on page 119 to find where Woof has buried some gold coins! The answer will be a letter and a number spelled out in letters. _ / _ _ _ _ _

MIX-UP MADNESS

What a muddle! Match the top halves of these characters
to the correct bottom halves.

MORE THINGS TO DO

* Imagine your own amazing fantasy characters and draw them in the two blank boxes!

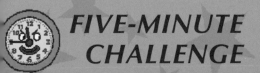

FIVE-MINUTE CHALLENGE

Write in some of the mixed-up characters' combination names, like "Vikingator" (Viking + gladiator)!

That was time well spent! Time-travel again back through the pages of Wenda's journey and discover even more things to see on the way.

BACK IN TIME CHECKLIST

- [ ] A yellow fan
- [ ] A cabbage thief
- [ ] An admiral saluting
- [ ] A cuckoo escaping
- [ ] A sideways hoop
- [ ] A snapped vine
- [ ] A dino-turtle
- [ ] A fallen tree
- [ ] A lion pyramid
- [ ] A sand pyramid
- [ ] A $50,000 reward
- [ ] Falling laundry
- [ ] A mermaid statue
- [ ] A masked woodcutter
- [ ] A red number 13
- [ ] A primitive fruit stand
- [ ] A fire-breathing gargoyle
- [ ] Four dinosaurs about to collide
- [ ] A caveman looking for a kiss
- [ ] Three shocked mastheads

MAGIC AND MYSTERY

GREETINGS, WONDROUS WANDERERS. JOIN ME ON A MAGICAL JAUNT BACK THROUGH LEGENDARY LANDS. WE SHALL FLY WITH DRAGONS, PUTTER THROUGH THE PAGES OF A STORYBOOK, AND PERHAPS EVEN BEHOLD MAGNIFICENT BEASTS OF OLD. IT'S SPELLBINDING!

SPELL-
BOUND

Color in Wizard
Whitebeard!

126

Make new things appear in the blank spaces on the
covers of Wizard Whitebeard's spell books!

127

FIVE-MINUTE CHALLENGE

Put down your wand and pick up your crayons! Color in all the stars to make them really magical.

DRAGON LORE

Color in all the dragons. Be as
imaginative as you like!

128

FIVE-MINUTE CHALLENGE **Can you name these dragons? Where are they coming from? Where are they going?**

129

MORE THINGS TO FIND

- ☐ Some upside-down arrows
- ☐ A walking stick
- ☐ Sixteen money bags

TWO BY TWO

Wizard Whitebeard is helping Noah get pairs of animals onto his ark. Connect the numbered red dots in order, and reveal a creature that wants to travel on its own.

FIVE-MINUTE CHALLENGE

MORE THINGS TO FIND
- [ ] An elephant-shaped tree
- [ ] Another Noah's Ark in this book
- [ ] A bird's nest
- [ ] A knot
- [ ] A warthog

DRAGON DELIGHT

A dragon flying competition is about to begin. Draw lots of other dragon contestants to take part in it!

MORE THINGS TO FIND

☐ A dragon with a very long tail

☐ A dragon egg

☐ A red-polka-dotted bag on a stick

131

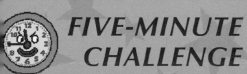

FIVE-MINUTE CHALLENGE

Name your magical dragons and add colorful dragons' eggs to the picture.

DRAGON MEDAL MAYHEM

What a day of exciting races! Can you match each dragon to the medal it won? Read all seven descriptions closely and study the pictures on the medals for clues.

HANSEL DUSTY

This greedy dragon likes anything shiny and has a good sense of smell (but very bad breath!).

Sneakiness: high

Sense of direction: high

Strength: big claws for grabbing

THE FORTY WINKS RACE

SUNNY-SIDE-UP SID

This happy-go-lucky dragon likes to see things from a different perspective.

Sneakiness: low

Sense of direction: low

Intelligence: not so smart!

THE NUMBER CRUNCHING RACE
52
49

EDWINA SHARP

This dreadfully competitive dragon has a bad temper and an extra-pointy arrow tail.

Top speed: very fast

Battle power: high

Strength: long claws to sharpen swords

THE NAVIGATION RACE

FIVE-MINUTE CHALLENGE

Dragons are excellent at riddles! Here are some real head (or scale!) scratchers:

• What is always in front of you but can never be seen?

CORNELIUS COMPASS

This witty dragon has sleek scales for aerodynamic tailwind.

Top speed: very fast

Sense of direction: exceptional; can read maps

Intelligence: high; likes to crack clever jokes!

THE UPSIDE-DOWN RACE

THE SWORD-FIGHTING RACE

COUNT BILL CRUNCH

This dragon is always hungry— for math!

Sneakiness: high

Strength: sharp fangs

Intelligence: high; can use his scales to count in multiples of nine

BUMP-IN-THE-NIGHT BERNIE

This scary dragon can float without flapping her wings. She likes to say "Boo!"

Sneakiness: exceptional; is a ghost

Strength: will grant wishes, if you can catch her

Intelligence: medium; can see through people

THE TREASURE HUNT RACE

THE NIGHT-FRIGHT RACE

SNOOZY VAN WINKLE

This toothless dragon prefers nighttime to day and can sleep for a year at a time.

Sense of direction: low

Tickle tolerance: low; giggles at the sight of feathers

Strength: raised yellow scales to soften the blow of bumping into things

- **Where can you find cities, mountains, forests, and roads but no people?**

- **What goes around the world without leaving its corner?**

FLYING HIGH

Time to visit the land of the dragon flyers!
Can you spot ten differences between the two pictures?

FIVE-MINUTE CHALLENGE

Unscramble these other
mysterious mystical creatures:

NUNORIC
NFIRIFG
IXHNPS

SPELL-TACULAR!

These four words have stretched out in a spectacular star shape.
Can you train your eyes to read them?

START HERE!

Clue: Hold the book in front of your nose where it says "Start Here." Read the word in front of you, then turn the book to the right and read the next word and so on.

FIVE-MINUTE CHALLENGE

THINGS TO FIND
- [ ] A white suitcase
- [ ] A striped rocket
- [ ] A green boot
- [ ] A frog

DRAGON FLYERS

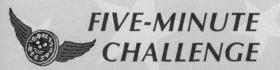

FIVE-MINUTE CHALLENGE

Imagine that *you're* a dragon flyer and you have a dragon of your own! Write down some of your adventures:

....

Color in this dragon delight!
Can you find a curly dragon tail?

GENIE-OUS!

Draw in the missing symbols to release the genie from its lamp! All nine symbols must appear once in each box, but never in the same row or column.

FIVE-MINUTE CHALLENGE

If you were granted three wishes, what would they be?

1: ....
2: ....
3: ....

TERRIFIC TRAVELS

Study the pictures of the extraordinary lands
Waldo has visited. How many of each item
listed next to each picture can you find?

Red birds:

_____

Pies thrown:

_____

Pairs of sunglasses:

_____

Green hoods:

_____

Yellow fish:

_____

Hats with feathers:

_____

Mustaches:

_____

FIVE-MINUTE CHALLENGE

MORE THINGS TO FIND
- ☐ Waldo's spare pair of glasses
- ☐ A red-and-yellow feather
- ☐ Odlaw in a Waldo hat
- ☐ A spider
- ☐ Fish eating boots

BRILLIANT BESTSELLERS

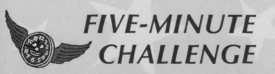

FIVE-MINUTE CHALLENGE

There are all sorts of colorful characters and creations hiding in this black-and-white scene!

Find and color in:
☐ A three-tiered cake
☐ A happy lion

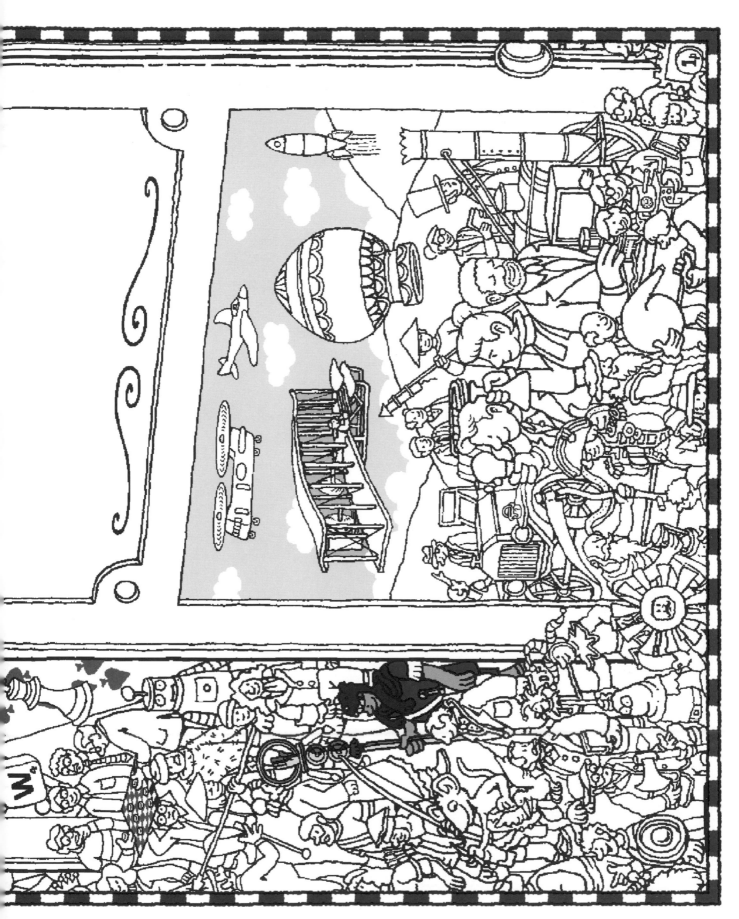

Think up titles for these books
and write them in!

- ☐ A playing card
- ☐ A harp
- ☐ Two airplanes
- ☐ A tentacled alien
- ☐ A giant mouse

WISE CRACKS

Wizard Whitebeard has cast a happy spell!
This scroll is inscribed with lots of jokes.
Which one makes you laugh the most?

HOW DO WIZARDS SET THE
TABLE FOR A TEA PARTY?

WITH CUPS AND
FLYING SORCERERS!

HOW MANY WIZARDS DOES IT TAKE
TO CAST A SPELL OF INVISIBILITY?

I DON'T KNOW, I CAN'T SEE THEM!

HOW CAN YOU DESCRIBE
A WIZARD'S BOOK?

SPELL-BINDING!

WHY CAN'T WIZARDS
CLEAN FLOORS?

BECAUSE THE WITCHES
STOLE THEIR BROOMS!

WHAT DID THE MAGICIAN DO
WHEN HE WAS VERY ANGRY?

HE PULLED HIS HARE OUT!

....

....

....

142

STARS AND STRIPES

Which path leads from Waldo's seal to the golden star? You'd better hurry, because there are multiple Waldos trying to reach it!

FIVE-MINUTE CHALLENGE

MORE THINGS TO FIND
- ☐ A hat with a blue pom-pom
- ☐ A Waldo who's taken off his hat
- ☐ A Waldo without glasses
- ☐ A striped walking stick

SHIELDS AND STAVES

En garde—eyes at the ready! Find two pictures that are the same.

GIANT GAME

Start on the board game square next to each player's picture.
Then follow each footstep guide to work out who gets the scroll.

MORE THINGS TO FIND

- [ ] Nine men wearing helmets
- [ ] Someone wearing blue-and-yellow tights
- [ ] Four pitchforks

FIVE-MINUTE CHALLENGE

Can you find another path to the scroll? Pick one character's starting square and add a new footstep guide.

- You must use at least six steps.
- You must change direction at least twice.

DOUBLE VISION

All is not what it seems with these magic monks and red-cloaked ghouls.
Spot six differences between these two scenes.

146

FIVE-MINUTE CHALLENGE Choose three characters from the scene, whether they're magic monks, gruesome ghouls, or stunning statues. Then draw in speech bubbles around the outside and add dialogue!

CREATURE FEATURE

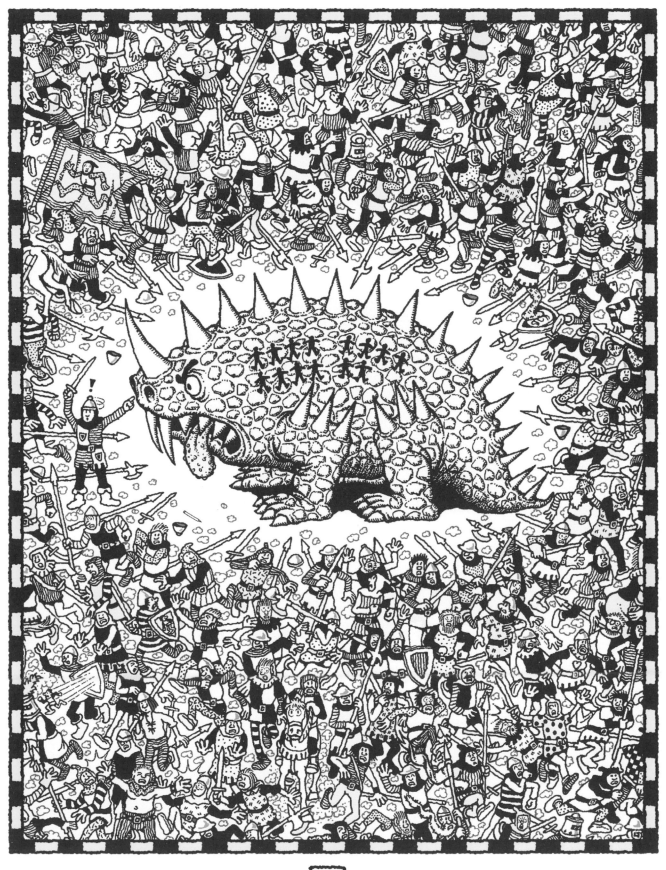

147

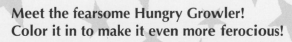

FIVE-MINUTE CHALLENGE

Meet the fearsome Hungry Growler!
Color it in to make it even more ferocious!

MONSTER MADNESS

Can you draw another monster in the middle of this scene? Make it as friendly or as terrifying as you like!

148

FIVE-MINUTE CHALLENGE

MORE THINGS TO DO
- Draw a crest on the white shield.

- Find twelve red-handled swords.
- Color in the white plume.
- Spot a dinosaur!

STRANGE CREATURE

Put Hungry Growler's face back together again by numbering the strips from 1 to 6.

FIVE-MINUTE CHALLENGE

What does Hungry Growler like to eat?
Breakfast: .... Lunch: ....
Dinner: ....

MONSTER MAYHEM

Yikes! Helmeted hunters are lost in a monstrous land!
What do you think they are saying, dreaming, singing, or yelling?

150

FIVE-MINUTE CHALLENGE

MORE THINGS TO FIND
- ☐ A jump rope
- ☐ A tickly tummy

- ☐ An artist at work
- ☐ A toothy cage
- ☐ A spear bridge

BITES & PIECES

Which three pieces are missing from the jigsaw puzzle? You have five pieces to choose from, so study each one carefully.

MORE THINGS TO FIND

☐ A dog-man holding two bones

☐ A cat on wheels

☐ A man dressed as a poodle

151

FIVE-MINUTE CHALLENGE

Using the pieces above as a guide, draw your own artwork in the gaps where the missing pieces are meant to be.

TOP FIENDS

Meet Odlaw's most ferocious team of fiends. Look at the pictures on the cards and match them to the correct description.

Name: Hungry Growler

Home: Swamp

Favorite Food: Everything and anything

Speed: Lumbering

Courage: 10

Spy Ability: 2

Fear Factor: 8

Special Skill: Roaring and emitting foul smells

Name: Heave-Ho Henry

Home: Dungeon

Favorite Food: Nuts and bolts

Speed: Slow when rusty

Courage: 4

Spy Ability: 9

Fear Factor: 10

Special Skill: Sneaking up on people

Name: Captain Cutlass

Home: The Black Skull

Favorite Food: Dried meats

Speed: Peg-leg slow

Courage: 9

Spy Ability: 6

Fear Factor: 6

Special Skill: Pillaging

Name: Warty Gretel

Home: The Witch's Castle

Favorite Food: Bats' tails, frogs' legs, eyes of a newt

Speed: Fast on a broom

Courage: 4

Spy Ability: 10

Fear Factor: 6

Special Skill: Potions and curses

Name: ....

Home: ....

Favorite Food: ....

Speed: ....

Courage: ....

Spy Ability: ....

Fear Factor: ....

Special Skill: ....

152

FIVE-MINUTE CHALLENGE

Create your own fiend and give it stats in the blank card above.

SWAMPY SWIRL

Read Odlaw's swampy, swirly message by turning the page counter-clockwise. Beware: the message is written backward!

MORE THINGS TO FIND

- [ ] A monster brushing its teeth
- [ ] A winged helmet
- [ ] A pair of snaky spectacles
- [ ] A man tied to a pole
- [ ] Three Odlaws wearing pink earmuffs
- [ ] A charmed snake

153

FIVE-MINUTE CHALLENGE

Find something else to spot in the scene, then create a series of clues for a friend to crack . . . backward!

....
....
....

ODLAW'S I-SPY!

Greetings, fellow troublemakers! I, Odlaw, love being a sneaky spy and spotting things on my vacations. Can you find all the things I've spotted in this spooky scene?

ODLAW'S I-SPY!

- [ ] A witch going the wrong way
- [ ] A witch riding upside down
- [ ] A dancing executioner
- [ ] A vampire holding a teddy bear
- [ ] A ghost train
- [ ] A sore finger
- [ ] A broom riding a witch
- [ ] Two prisoners catching two executioners
- [ ] A vampire holding a bat

154

FIVE-MINUTE CHALLENGE

Make your own checklist of things to find in the world around you! Here are a few to start:

- [ ] A storm cloud
- [ ] A red traffic light
- [ ] An ice-cream cone

WHICH WITCH IS WHICH?

Read the witchy riddles and match them to the pictures.

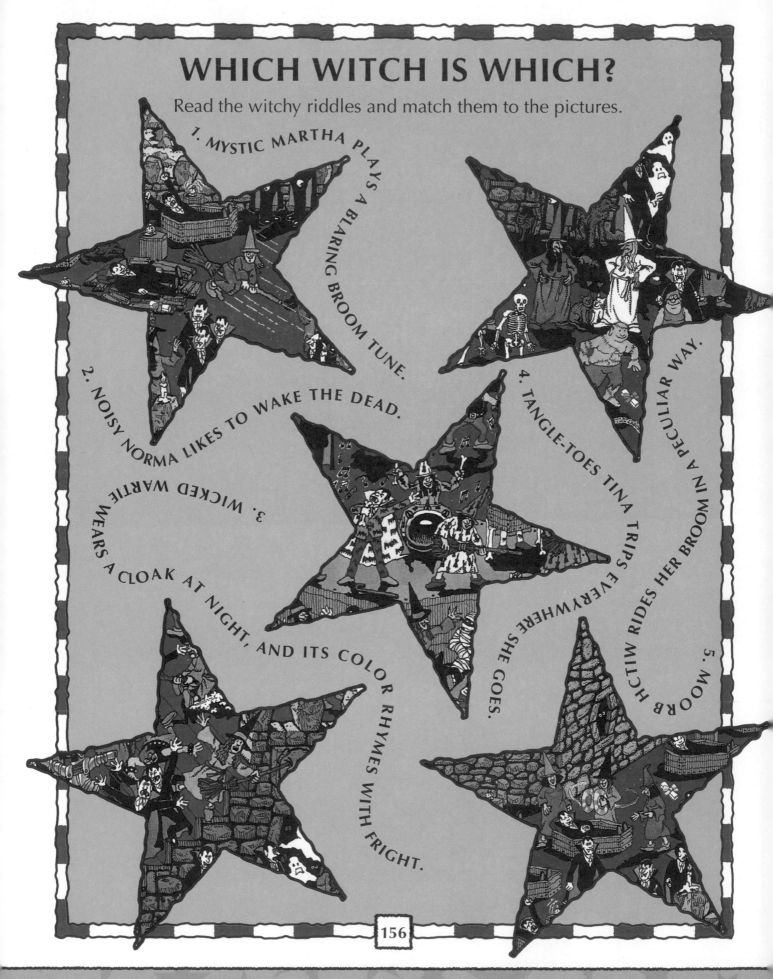

1. MYSTIC MARTHA PLAYS A BLARING BROOM TUNE.

2. NOISY NORMA LIKES TO WAKE THE DEAD.

3. WICKED WARTIE WEARS A CLOAK AT NIGHT, AND ITS COLOR RHYMES WITH FRIGHT.

4. TANGLE-TOES TINA TRIPS EVERYWHERE SHE GOES.

5. MOORB HCTIW RIDES HER BROOM IN A PECULIAR WAY.

156

FIVE-MINUTE CHALLENGE

Can you crack these codes about other characters in these scenes?
1. Toothy Tony belted into the microbone.
2. Frankenstein Fred spied a scroll.

CONNECT THE BONES

Can you connect all nine bones by using only four straight lines? You may not lift your pencil off the page, but your lines may go outside the grid.

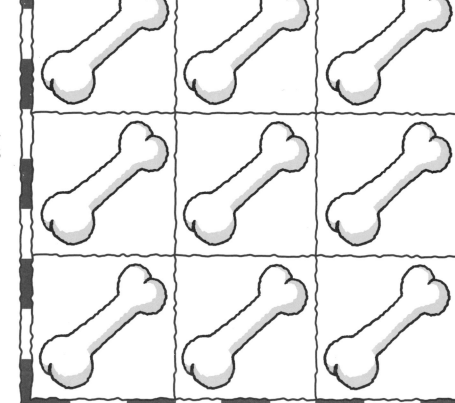

FIVE-MINUTE CHALLENGE

Join the bones by four lines, taking your pencil off the paper once. How many squares are there in the grid? Don't forget that the outer box is a square, and four grid boxes also make a square!

BIRD SEARCH WORD SEARCH

Find the name of each feathered flying friend in this frame of letters. The words go forward, backward, and diagonally. Squawk!

O	O	K	C	U	C	W	D	P
U	R	C	V	B	O	K	R	V
M	E	D	L	R	O	M	I	U
E	K	A	C	T	I	W	B	L
W	C	R	G	L	A	A	G	T
	E	W	E	L	B	G	N	U
R	P	I	D	G	E	T	I	R
C	D	O	U	N	O	A	K	E
N	O	V	E	O	M	I	C	W
U	O	R	K	C	W	L	O	
A	W	D	L	L	U	G	M	

Word list:
- Eagle
- Wren • Gull
- Crow • Cuckoo
- Mockingbird
- Woodpecker
- Wagtail
- Vulture
- Emu

MORE THINGS TO FIND

- [ ] The word *Odlaw*
- [ ] An upside-down pom-pom hat
- [ ] A dinosaur
- [ ] A very long snake
- [ ] Five monkeys
- [ ] Four bats
- [ ] Two witches
- [ ] Sixty-six yellow-and-black-striped birds

158

FIVE-MINUTE CHALLENGE

The letter *W* has been taken out of each of these bird names. Can you add it back in the right place?
SPARRO   OL   HAK   ARBLER   SAN

MAGNIFIED MISCHIEF

Which one of Odlaw's magnifying lenses reveals
striped snakes, birds, and monkeys?

MORE THINGS TO FIND

- ☐ Two gold crowns
- ☐ Three broken spears
- ☐ Eleven blue hats
- ☐ A snake staff
- ☐ A pirate hat
- ☐ Eleven piranhas

MENACING MUG SHOT

Imagine you're a brilliant detective and you've just brought in your chief suspect. Fill in their rap sheet below and draw their mug shot!

$10,000

CRIMINAL RECORD

Name: ....

....

Date of Arrest: ....

Confession*:   YES   /   NO

Hair*: Black / Brown / Blond / Red / Green / Bald

Eyes*: Brown / Blue / Green / Hazel / Purple / Yellow

*CIRCLE AS RELEVANT

Details of Crime: ....

....

....

....

THINGS TO THINK ABOUT

✎ How did you catch them?

✎ Do they have any distinctive features?

✎ Do they have any special skills?

160

FIVE-MINUTE CHALLENGE

Find a partner to play a suspect for you to interrogate . . . but with a twist! They cannot use the words *yes* or *no* in their answers to your questions. Can you crack them? Swap roles when they slip up!

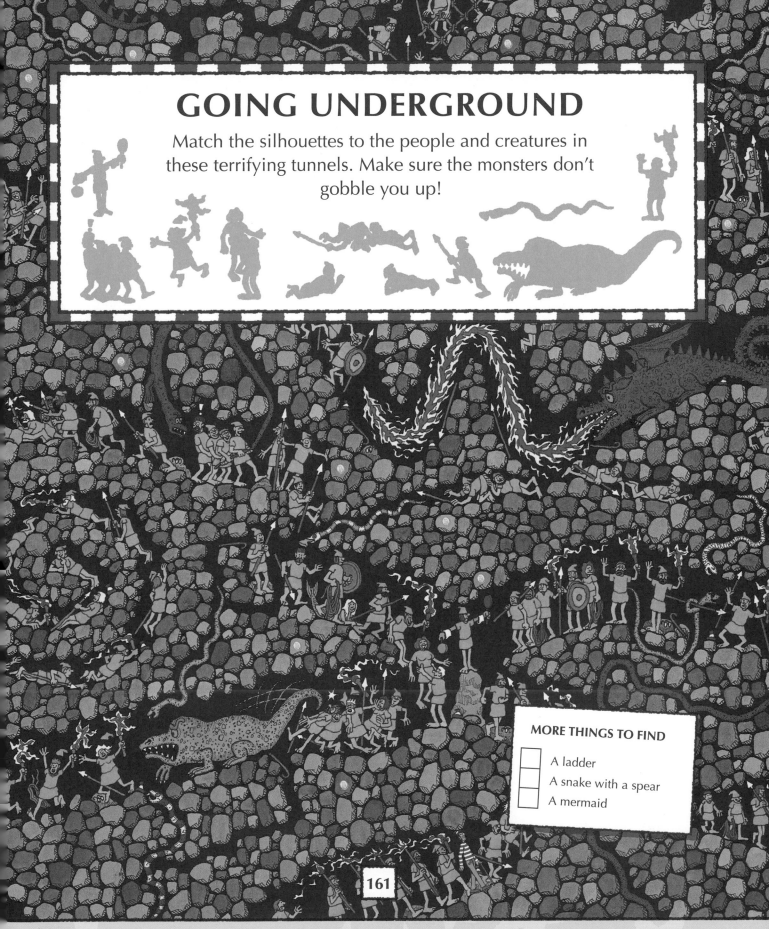

GOING UNDERGROUND

Match the silhouettes to the people and creatures in these terrifying tunnels. Make sure the monsters don't gobble you up!

MORE THINGS TO FIND

- A ladder
- A snake with a spear
- A mermaid

161

FIVE-MINUTE CHALLENGE

Odlaw's hidden a host of gold coins in this underground cave. Can you find all ten of them?

SNAKING WORDS

Read the clues and work out the answers by connecting the letters inside each frame without taking your pen off the paper!

1. Clue: A sea-traveling invader

N I
G K
V I

2. Clue: A sword-swishing soldier

E T E
K M E
S U R

3. Clue: A skeletal symbol used by pirates

K S S E B S
U A N N O S
L L D C R O

MORE THINGS TO FIND

☐ Nine yellow-headed birds

☐ Three vampires

☐ A flying witch

FIVE-MINUTE CHALLENGE Make your own snaky word and challenge a friend to crack it!

DISGUISE, DISGUISE!

Color in the Odlaws!

Spot something wrong with the pattern on the frame!

163

Oh, no! Here are twelve Odlaws. But which is the real one? Figure it out as quickly as possible!

That was magic! Gaze back through Wizard Whitebeard's adventure and see if you can reveal these extraordinary items.

MAGIC AND MYSTERY CHECKLIST

- [ ] A pink potion
- [ ] A cat on wheels
- [ ] Feather swords
- [ ] A corkscrew tail
- [ ] A snake reading a book
- [ ] A sparkling-clean tail
- [ ] A catapult
- [ ] A pair of gorillas
- [ ] A green boot
- [ ] A game of checkers
- [ ] A game of human chess
- [ ] A sunny painting
- [ ] Coffin bowling
- [ ] A flag trying to run away
- [ ] A pair of spotted orange leggings
- [ ] A dog wearing sunglasses
- [ ] Two blue pinstriped suits
- [ ] A wizard hat with green stars
- [ ] Wizard Whitebeard playing the violin

SPACE STATION

WELCOME, FIENDS AND FOES. I'M HERE TO TAKE YOU ON A DASTARDLY TRIP OUT OF THIS WORLD. OH YES, THIS GRUESOME GALAXY IS FILLED WITH SPACESHIPS, STRANGE PLANETS, ALIEN LIFE, AND EVEN SOME EXTRATERRESTRIAL TERRORS, SO BEWARE!

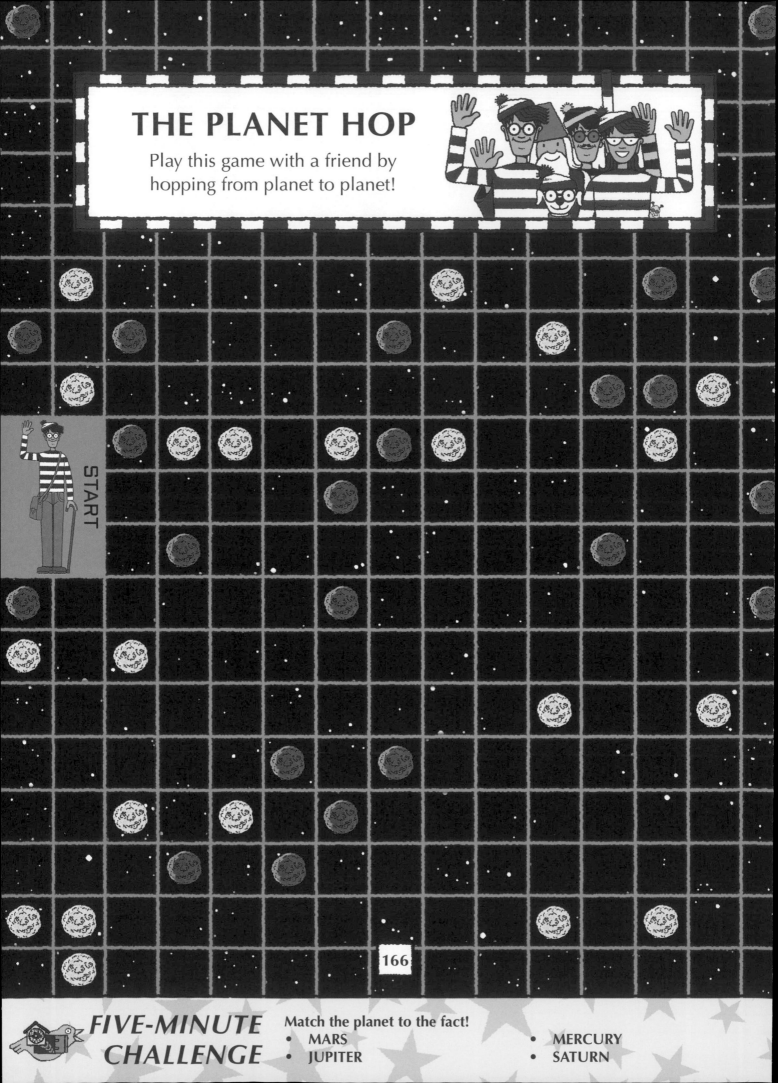

THE PLANET HOP

Play this game with a friend by hopping from planet to planet!

START

166

FIVE-MINUTE CHALLENGE

Match the planet to the fact!
- MARS
- JUPITER

- MERCURY
- SATURN

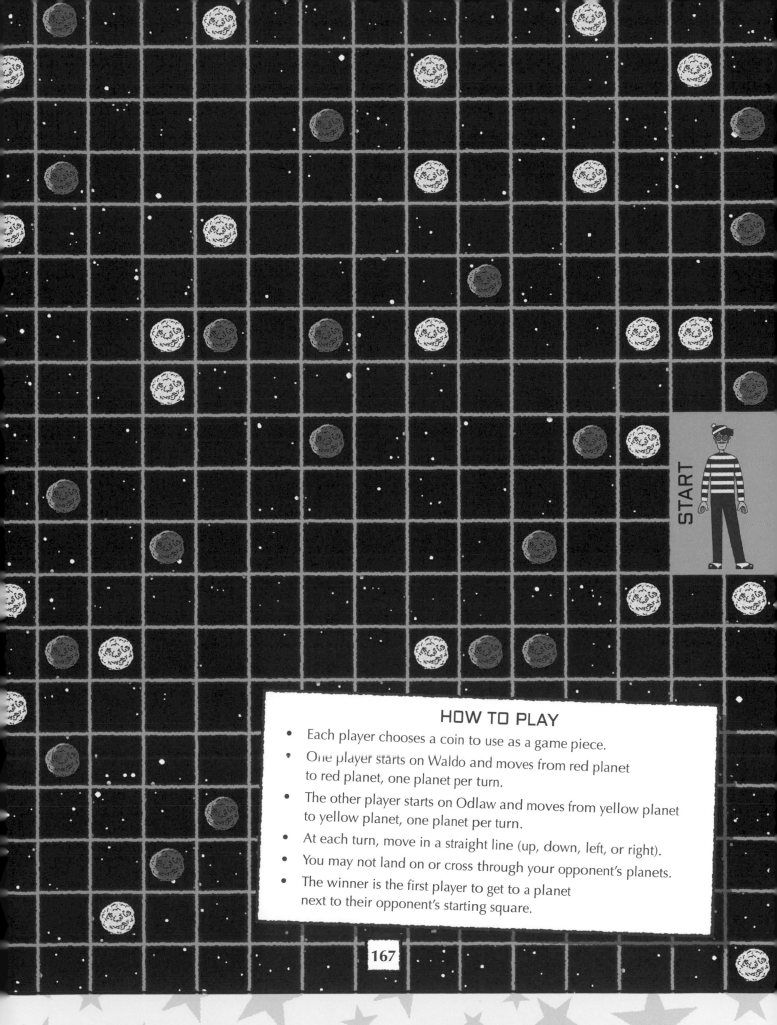

START

HOW TO PLAY

- Each player chooses a coin to use as a game piece.
- One player starts on Waldo and moves from red planet to red planet, one planet per turn.
- The other player starts on Odlaw and moves from yellow planet to yellow planet, one planet per turn.
- At each turn, move in a straight line (up, down, left, or right).
- You may not land on or cross through your opponent's planets.
- The winner is the first player to get to a planet next to their opponent's starting square.

- I'm known as the red planet.
- I am the fastest-spinning planet in the solar system.

- I have 62 moons.
- A year on my planet is 88 days in Earth time.

MOON-MAZE MAYHEM

Help Waldo find a path through the moon to reach the red star.

MORE THINGS TO FIND

☐ A horseshoe

☐ Five green aliens

☐ A question mark

☐ An exclamation mark

FIVE-MINUTE CHALLENGE

Find out the scientific names for these constellations!
The Great Bear: ....

The Flying Horse: ....
The Hunter: ....

MOON MUDDLE

Help stop the hullabaloo on the planet of red and blue! Find the words in the moon of letters. The words go up, down, forward, and backward.

ORBIT
SPACE SUIT
ROBOT
VOYAGER
CRATER
PULSAR

FIVE-MINUTE CHALLENGE

But wait! There are more words to find:
- ☐ Wormhole
- ☐ Sunspot
- ☐ Jetpack
- ☐ Dust
- ☐ Full moon
- ☐ Nova

TELEPORTATION TANGLE

What a tangle! Follow the teleportation rays to find out who's traveling where.

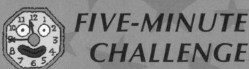

FIVE-MINUTE CHALLENGE

See the books that Waldo's holding? How many are there? Make up some space-tastic titles for them!

SPACE STATION DUPLICATION

Can you spot ten differences between these two scenes?

FIVE-MINUTE CHALLENGE

Would you rather:
- Live on another planet or live under the sea?
- Be an astronaut or an alien?
- Experience zero gravity or see a real UFO?

SPACE STATION REPLICATION

Can you spot ten differences between the scenes?

FIVE-MINUTE CHALLENGE

How many times does this character appear elsewhere in this section? Find as many of them as you can in five minutes!

ALIEN INVASION

173

STAR GAZE DAZE

Pair up any stars with pictures that seem similar and then spot the three differences between each pair. It's extra eye-boggling!

FIVE-MINUTE CHALLENGE

Wenda loves the music of the stars. Can you find nine stars shaped like musical notes?

WANDERING LINES

Look at all those blue Martians! Mark all the places where you can find three matching boxes in a row. They can be straight or diagonal. Odlaw found one already!

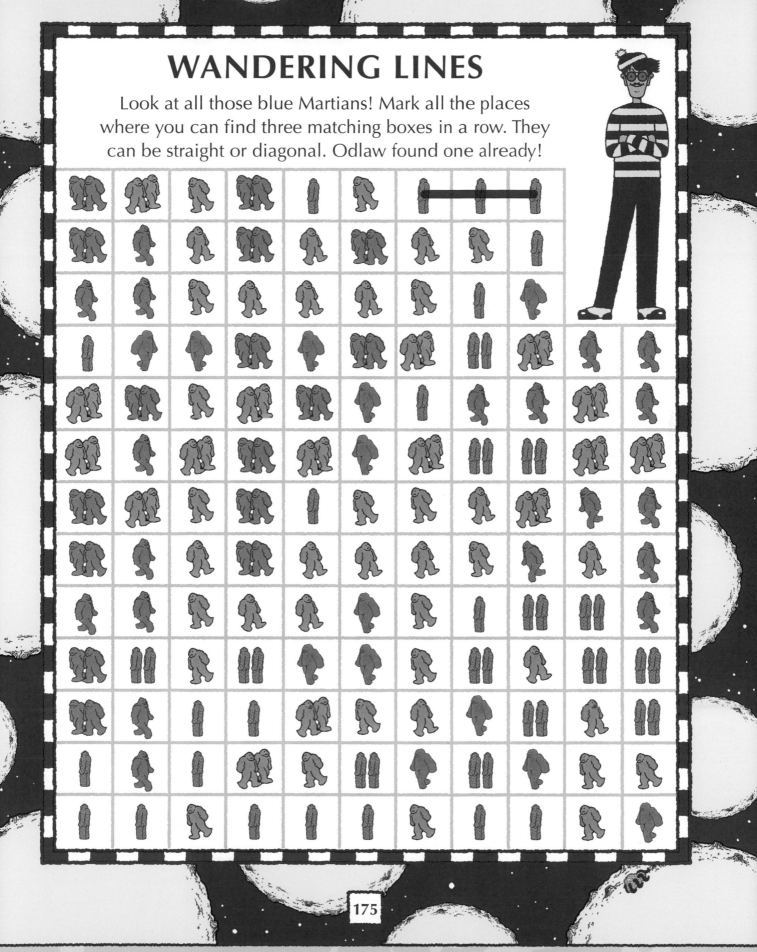

175

MAKING CONTACT

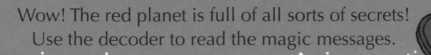

Wow! The red planet is full of all sorts of secrets!
Use the decoder to read the magic messages.

A B C D E F G H I J K L M N O P Q R S T U V W X Y Z

FIVE-MINUTE CHALLENGE

Use the code to write secret messages for your friends to decipher!

WORD WORLDS

Gravity has made mayhem of these words!
Read the clues to help you unscramble the letters.

1. Another word for alien
R A R X
E I X L
T E I T
R A

2. Its size is unknown
U R E
S
E N V I

3. It's really big
P A
S E C

4. Orbits Earth
O M
N O

5. Something that orbits another object
I L T S L
A E
T E E

6. Drives a spacecraft
N S A U
A
T O T R

7. Called the "Red Planet"
M S
A R

8. Lights up Earth
U S
N

9. Star shine
T N W I
L K
E E

10. Instrument with glass lenses
E S C T L
O
P E E

11. Has a tail
M T O
C E

12. Our galaxy (two words)
A M K
Y I K
W Y L

177

MORE THINGS TO DO
* Spot a blue Martian who is asleep on a rock!

HALF ALIEN, HALF . . .

What a bunch of crazy-looking creatures!
Can you pair up their top and bottom halves?

FIVE-MINUTE CHALLENGE

Use a pencil and paper to trace this page, then cut out the
characters' top and bottom halves to make new mixed-up creatures!

BLASTOFF

179

FIVE-MINUTE CHALLENGE   Color in this rad rocket. Then give all the crew members supersonic names!

SPACE MAIL

Whoops! What an intergalactic mailroom mix-up!
Match each message to a stamp to find out
who did (and who didn't) send postcards.

TODAY I MET WOOF AND WENDA WAITING WITH ALIENS AT A SPACESHIP STOP. ONE OF THE ALIENS WAS WEARING A RED-POM-POM HAT—JUST LIKE MINE! WOW! WISH YOU WERE HERE!

WALDO-WATCHERS WANDERING ABOUT, PLANET EARTH, THE UNIVERSE

Zip-zap-swoosh-boing! I cast a magic spell to make a rocket! Can you believe my beard got caught in its antenna and I was carried light-years away?

Waldo

Walking Here and There,

With a Walking Stick,

Wherever You Are

180

FIVE-MINUTE CHALLENGE Once you've matched the space mail to the sender, copy their image into the postmark!

I'M FEELING BLUE TODAY, AND NOT JUST IN COLOR. MY BROTHER (HE STICKS HIS TONGUE OUT A LOT!) WON'T TAKE ME TO HIS SPACEBALL MATCH ON PLANET ZOG. CAN YOU MAKE IT HAPPEN?

MAKE A WISH COME TRUE INC.

LUCKY LETTERBOX,

SHOOTING STAR CITY

I SNOOZED IN THE SOLAR HAMMOCK YOU SENT ME AND FLOATED TOO CLOSE TO THE SUN. I'M NOT ORANGE ANYMORE AND MY THREE EYES ARE SORE! OUCH!

MOM

RED STAR STREET,

NEAR THE BLACK HOLE,

BESIDE PLANET WHOOPSY

RIDDLE ME THIS,
RIDDLE ME THAT,

I'M SNEAKING ABOUT LIKE A BLACK CYBER CAT.

I HAVE SUNGLASSES AND A MUSTACHE FOR MY DISGUISE.

TRY TO TRACK DOWN MY YELLOW-AND-BLACK ALIEN ALLIES!

TOP SECRET
NOWHERE,
EVERYWHERE,
PLANET HIDE-AND-SEEK

181

FIVE-MINUTE CHALLENGE

Create your own out-of-this-world stamp in the blank space!

SATELLITE SETS

Wow, it's crowded up here at night! Can you match each object in the sky with one or more identical copies—and reveal the one thing that is flying solo?

FIVE-MINUTE CHALLENGE Here's a totally cool comet game! You will need: aluminum foil (for comets), a cup or other container (to be a black hole), and a little bit of space!

MORE THINGS TO FIND

- [ ] Six yellow cars
- [ ] Two fish
- [ ] Six thermometers
- [ ] Eighteen striped planets
- [ ] Two astronauts with wrenches

To play: Tear the foil into random-sized chunks and scrunch them up into balls. Stand a distance from your cup, and try to toss your comets in one at a time. See how small you can make your comet and still get it in!

Odlaw's mission isn't quite accomplished! Launch yourself back into space and scope out these intergalactic sights.

SPACE STATION CHECKLIST

- [ ] An extraterrestrial line
- [ ] An alien with twelve fingers and twelve toes
- [ ] A starry bear in a red sky
- [ ] A red flag
- [ ] Pyramids
- [ ] A rope bridge
- [ ] Green boots
- [ ] A yellow biplane
- [ ] A monochrome lightbulb alien
- [ ] A lightbulb alien in full color
- [ ] An airborne alien fight
- [ ] A lizard crew member
- [ ] A cat with three eyes
- [ ] A smiling blue planet
- [ ] An air-traffic collision
- [ ] An alien with four pink legs
- [ ] An alien with a belly button
- [ ] Six yellow planets with matching rings
- [ ] Seven crescent moons
- [ ] An alien wearing sunglasses

WHO'S WHO?

What a mix-up! Unscramble the anagrams and fill in the boxes next to them. Then draw a line to match the pictures to your answers.

OWOF	
GIMNCIAA	
DALWO	
LDOWA AWCTERH	
VEMCANA	
IPARET	
RIOSNDAU	
CTAROAB	
IGHNKT	
GIKINV	

FIVE-MINUTE CHALLENGE   Write an anagram of your name in the empty space above!

CAKE-TASTROPHE!

Help Wenda figure out all the ingredients for this cake recipe by crossing out the letters in gray that spell Wenda in every word.

WSEUGNADRA
WBEUNTTDEAR
EWGENGDAS
FWLENODAUR
VWANEILLNA EDXTRAACT
BWAEKING NPODWDAER

MORE THINGS TO FIND

- ☐ A gingerbread person
- ☐ Wenda's cake with three red layers
- ☐ A double-ended wooden spoon

187

FIVE-MINUTE CHALLENGE

Can you crack these extra ingredients?
- CWHOECONLADTEA
- WECRENAMDA
- WECINNNDAMON

WHO DONUT?

Someone has eaten Waldo's birthday cake! Who could it have been? Read the testimonies below, then see if you can guess who the crumb-filled culprit is.

IT WAS A BEAUTIFUL SUNNY SUNDAY, SO I WENT FOR A BIRTHDAY STROLL, THEN CAME BACK TO MEET MY PALS FOR THE PARTY. BY THE TIME I ARRIVED, THE CAKE WAS ALREADY GONE!

I was wrapping Waldo's birthday present, which is tricky when you only have paws! I asked Odlaw for help when he snuck past, but he said he was busy. By the time I was ready to fetch the cake, there were only crumbs left. . . .

✎ Draw the correct flag in this box.

188

There are lots of fantastic flags from around the world in the background of this scene. Study them carefully and find out which countries they represent.

I WAS OUT AT THE POST OFFICE PICKING UP WALDO'S BIRTHDAY CARDS AND PRESENTS. BY THE TIME I GOT BACK, THE PARTY HAD ALREADY STARTED, AND THE CAKE WAS GONE. I BET THEY ALL ATE THE CAKE TOGETHER WHILE I WAS AWAY!

I was in my magical workshop all morning making a birthday surprise for Waldo. Odlaw popped in to see if he could help, but I said no—it's not a good idea to let someone so diabolical near my spell books!

I SPENT THE MORNING HANGING UP DECORATIONS FOR THE PARTY. THE CAKE WAS IN THE KITCHEN NEXT DOOR. I THINK I MIGHT HAVE HEARD THE DOOR OPEN AND CLOSE, BUT I WAS TOO BUSY BLOWING UP BALLOONS TO GO CHECK!

189

But wait—one flag is wrong! Once you've found it, draw it correctly in the blank space.

FOOD COLORING

FIVE-MINUTE CHALLENGE

What a yummy, scrummy cake factory!
Find the following things and color them in with
crazy colors as quickly as possible.

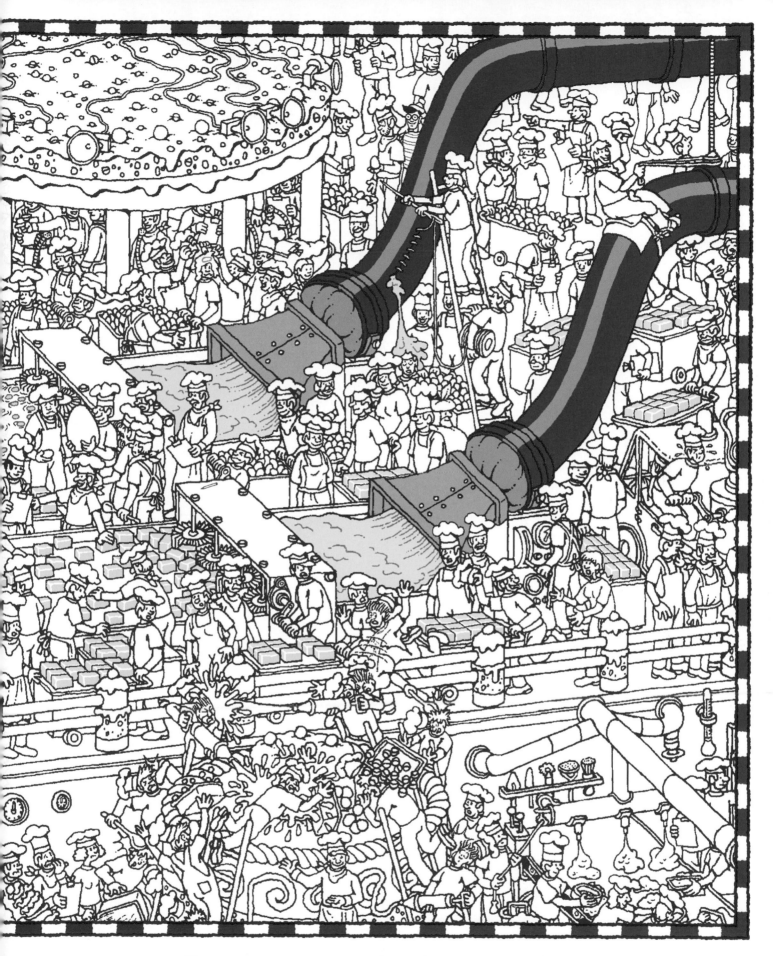

Create as many crazy cake colors as you can!

MORE THINGS TO FIND
- [ ] An egg-and-spoon race
- [ ] A cake stand
- [ ] A burnt cake
- [ ] Someone slipping on a stick of butter
- [ ] A thermometer

BALLOON BEDLAM

What a terrific tangle! Follow the strings to find out which balloons Waldo and his friends are holding.

192

Look at the patterns in the border to find a sequence that matches the order of the patterns on the balloons. Then color in the pattern on the empty balloon.

DOTTY DOT-TO-DOT

Connect all the even-numbered dots in order, and find out
what curiously shaped balloons are floating in the sky.

MORE THINGS TO FIND

☐ Seven cream pies

☐ Eleven blue bow ties

☐ Two clowns wearing the
same hat

193

Color in your clown-town creations and draw in more passengers!

FRIEND FRENZY

FIVE-MINUTE CHALLENGE

So many friends have come for the big party! Quick as you can, color in:

- All the animal pals
- Everyone wearing a hat
- The palm tree

FIVE-MINUTE CHALLENGE

Choose names for some of the characters from the scene above, then make a guest list!

....
....
....

HOT-AIR RACE

Clowns don't like to follow rules! Read the rules on the right to figure out which hot-air balloon is winning and which ones are disqualified. You'll go oogly-boogly-woogly-eyed!

196

FIVE-MINUTE CHALLENGE

Here are three kooky clown facts with some key information missing. Find out what it is and fill in the blanks!
• A fear of clowns is called ....

To enter the race:

- A hot-air balloon must have a crew of three clowns and no one else.

- One clown must wear a bow tie.

- A second clown must wear a top hat.

- A third clown must wear a red nose.

- Stripes and spots cannot be worn by the same clown.

- No pies allowed!

- A hot-air balloon basket must be the shape of a pom-pom hat.

197

- **National Clown Week was first made official by President** ....
- **Clowns traditionally have** .... **noses.**

HALL OF MIRRORS

In one of these mirrors, Waldo is facing in the opposite direction from the way he's facing in the other three. Can you spot which one?

MORE THINGS TO FIND

- [ ] A yellow flower squirting water
- [ ] A punch-in-the-box
- [ ] Someone wearing a chef's hat

198

FIVE-MINUTE CHALLENGE Try this game with your friends! One person makes a funny face. The next person copies it, then makes a new one. The next makes the first funny face, then the second, then makes another. Take turns until someone makes a mistake!

SUPER SWARM

Find five floating balloons with the correct pictures of Waldo and his friends on them (for Woof, all you can see is his tail—it has five red stripes!)

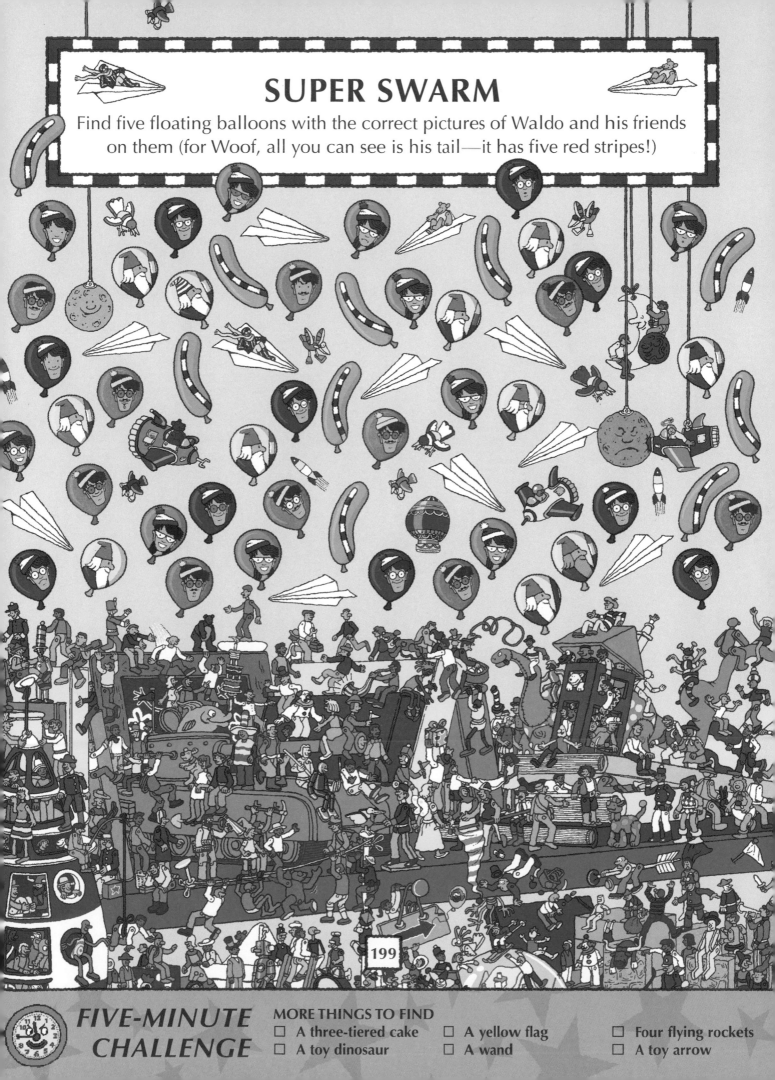

FIVE-MINUTE CHALLENGE

MORE THINGS TO FIND

- [ ] A three-tiered cake
- [ ] A toy dinosaur
- [ ] A yellow flag
- [ ] A wand
- [ ] Four flying rockets
- [ ] A toy arrow

WILD AND WACKY Ws

Can you fit all of the *W* words in the puzzle? One of the words has *wandered* backward, and another doesn't begin with *W* but is all over.

WAHOO

WAVE

WHOOPEE

WHOOSH

WONDER

EVERYWHERE

WEB

WHIZZ

WITTY

WILD

WOW

WIG

REDNAW

WISE

WACKY

WAVE

200

SNAKES AND LADDERS

Waldo and Odlaw are playing snakes and ladders!
Follow the instructions to work out who wins.

HOW TO PLAY

○ Have Odlaw and Waldo take turns, each time moving the number of squares indicated by their "dice roll" shown at right.

○ So Odlaw goes first, moving two squares, then Waldo goes, moving four squares, and so on.

○ If a player's turn ends on a square at the bottom of a ladder, he should go up it.

○ If a turn ends on a square with a snake's head, the player slides down it.

○ The winner is the player who lands on square number 30 first.

MORE THINGS TO DO

Find a die and play your own game of snakes and ladders with your friends.

201

FIVE-MINUTE CHALLENGE

Try the game again with a friend, only this time imagine you go up snakes and down ladders. What if one person only goes up snakes and the other person only goes up ladders? See who wins!

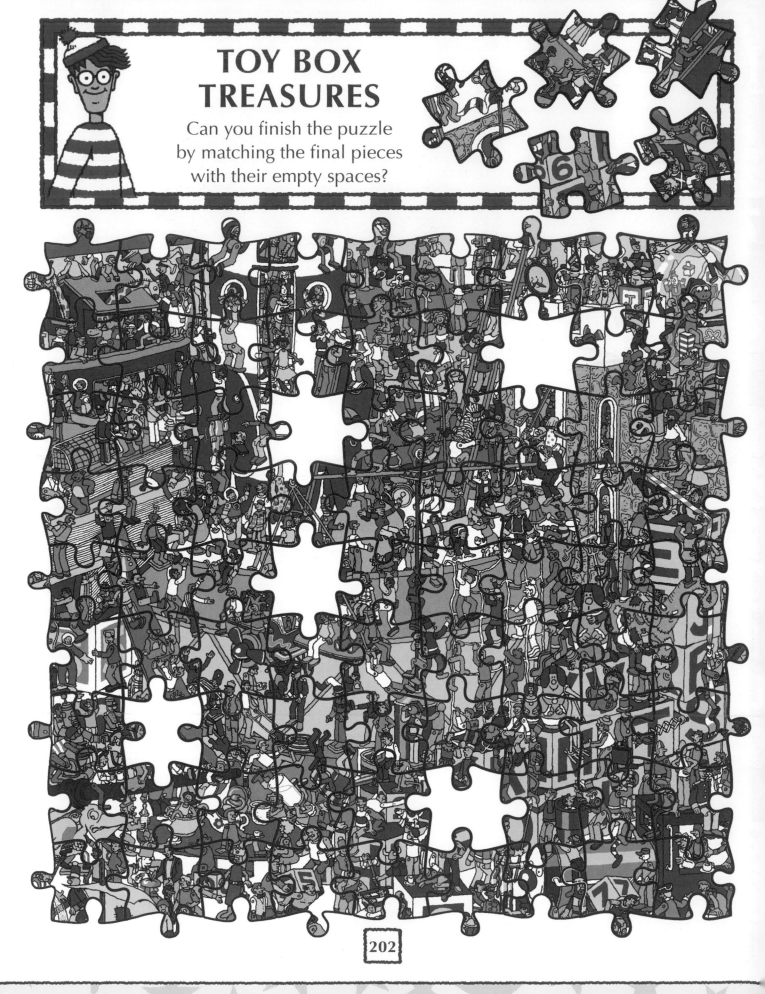

TOY BOX TREASURES

Can you finish the puzzle by matching the final pieces with their empty spaces?

202

MORE THINGS TO FIND
- ☐ A baby with a big lollipop
- ☐ A zebra climbing a ladder
- ☐ A waving astronaut
- ☐ A wind-up chicken
- ☐ A bumblebee

MAGIC NUMBER

Cross out the numbers in the border matching these descriptions and reveal a magic number.

☆ **All the sevens**

☆ **Any two numbers next to each other that are the same**

☆ **Any two numbers next to each other that add up to ten**

☆ **Even numbers**

MORE THINGS TO FIND

☐ Eleven bears
☐ A kangaroo
☐ Two astronauts
☐ A magic star wand

FIVE-MINUTE CHALLENGE

If you add up all the numbers in the border, you get 359! Using only five numbers of your choice, try to get as close as possible to the same total again. Add, divide, subtract, or multiply the numbers to get there.

BUSY BANDSTAND

What a musical muddle! Look at the clapper board and match up the instruments with the items or pieces used to play them.

DRUM	
CLARINET	MOUTHPIECE
GUITAR	BOW
TROMBONE	KEYS
VIOLIN	ROD
TRIANGLE	PICK
PIANO	REED
	STICKS

FIVE-MINUTE CHALLENGE Find animal costumes in the scene beginning with the letters *B*, *C*, *P*, and *R*.

UNDER THE SPOTLIGHT

Lights, camera, action! Can you spot ten differences between these two musical stage scenes?

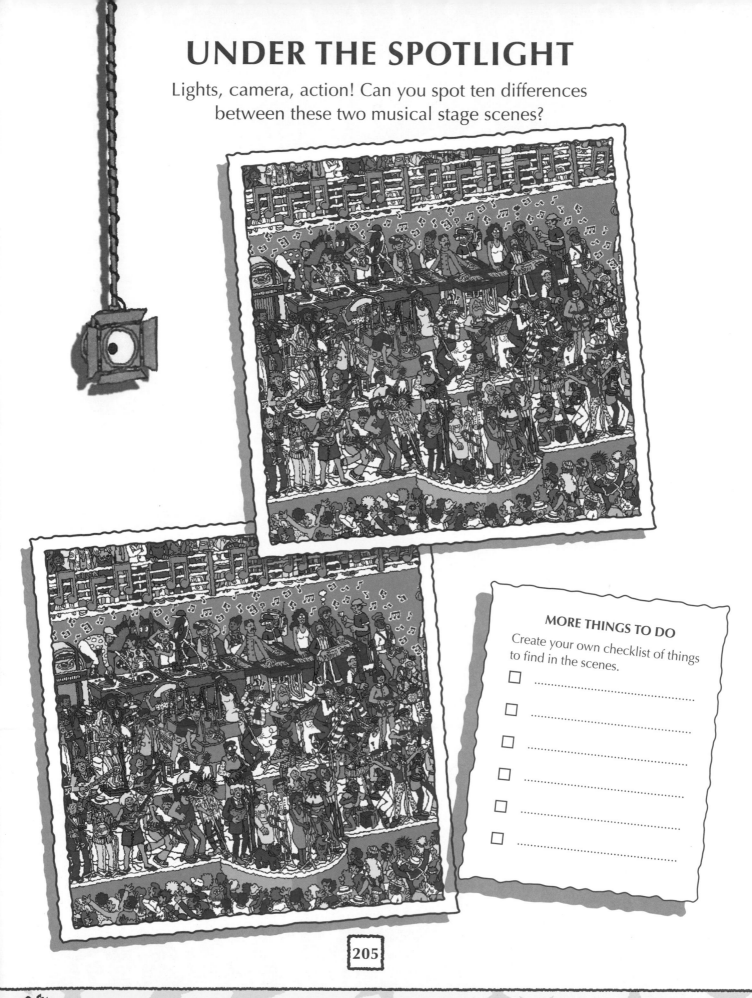

MORE THINGS TO DO

Create your own checklist of things to find in the scenes.

☐ ....

☐ ....

☐ ....

☐ ....

☐ ....

☐ ....

FIVE-MINUTE CHALLENGE

Find another scene in the book and have a friend make you a checklist! Too easy? Instead of the actual names of things, try writing cryptic clues!

A COLORFUL TUNE

Can you find these sets of musical notes inside the grid?
The answers run across, down, and diagonally.

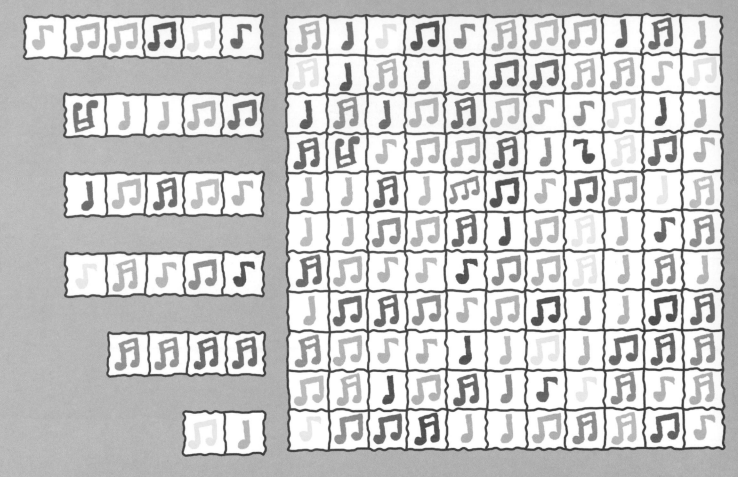

FIVE-MINUTE CHALLENGE

MORE THINGS TO FIND
- ☐ A man looking through a porthole
- ☐ A backward note in the grid
- ☐ Ten musical T-shirts
- ☐ Five trumpets
- ☐ A man in a drum

DANCING SILHOUETTES

Wenda has sent you a postcard from her party. Match the silhouettes with her funky-stepping friends on the dance floor.

I'M HAVING SUCH A GREAT TIME PLAYING MY FAVORITE TUNES, AND LOTS OF PEOPLE ARE BUSTING THEIR BEST MOVES ON THE DANCE FLOOR! HERE ARE THE BEST ONES SO FAR . . .

WENDA

FIVE-MINUTE CHALLENGE

Five letters are hidden in this scene that spell out Wenda's favorite dance. Clue: The word starts with the first letter of her name.

_ _ _ _ _

FOND FAREWELL

Fill this scene with color!

The party isn't over yet! Boogie back through these fun-filled pages and find even more things to entertain you.

THE ULTIMATE PARTY CHECKLIST

- [ ] A green dinosaur
- [ ] Carrot drumsticks
- [ ] A cake lifter
- [ ] An accordion
- [ ] A giant egg
- [ ] A man stuck in a faucet
- [ ] A conga line
- [ ] A clown skiing
- [ ] Steel drummers
- [ ] A soccer ball
- [ ] A police officer
- [ ] A tightrope walker
- [ ] A robot dog
- [ ] A waving gingerbread person
- [ ] A clown mummy
- [ ] Two newspapers
- [ ] People mixing music
- [ ] A saw-fish
- [ ] A green snake wearing a red hat
- [ ] A rabbit coming out of a hat

CONGRATULATIONS! YOU'VE REACHED THE END OF THIS BLOCKBUSTER SET OF BRAIN BUSTERS! DID YOU SOLVE ALL THE PUZZLES? COMPLETE ALL THE COLORING? FIND EVERYTHING THERE IS TO SPOT AND TRY OUT EVERY FIVE-MINUTE CHALLENGE? WELL DONE! BUT THERE'S MORE. EVERY FIVE-MINUTE CHALLENGE CLOCK APPEARS MORE THAN ONCE, APART FROM ONE. CAN YOU SPOT THE ODD CLOCK OUT?

TOO EASY? WHY NOT TIME YOURSELF . . . SAY, FIVE MINUTES?

Waldo

ANSWERS

p. 6 TRAVEL ESSENTIALS

MORE THINGS TO DO

cera rac = race car; dgrna iapno = grand piano;
ckhneti snki = kitchen sink

p. 7 COSTUME COSTS

1 hat	$1
1 tie	$2
1 tie	$2
1 shirt	$3
1 shirt	$3
1 jacket	$4
	= $15

p. 9 TRAVEL TWISTER

					P	A	S	S	P	O	R	T		
S	U	I	T	C	A	S	E							
												L		
		W				J	O	U	R	N	E	Y		
M	A									V				
A	L			O		T	A	O	B	A				
P	K			D						R				
I	I			L						T				
N	N			A		C	A	R						
G	G			W										
T	S						W	O	O	F				
R	T	C	A	M	E	R	A							
A	I				E	N	A	L	P					
I	C													
N	K													

p. 10 DESTINATION EVERYWHERE

Waldo went from New York to São Paulo to Rome to Toyko. Wenda went from London to Sydney. Woof went from Hong Kong to Paris. Wizard Whitebeard left from Amsterdam but missed his flight in Toronto. Odlaw left from Oslo but missed his flight in Dubai.

FIVE-MINUTE CHALLENGE
Toenail

p. 11 TRANSPORT TANGLE

pp. 12–13 RUNAWAY RUNWAY

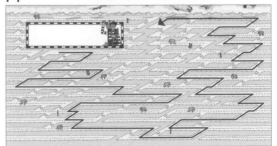

p. 16 LOST LUGGAGE

FIVE-MINUTE CHALLENGE
toothpaste; camera; stamps; teddy bear; diary; sunglasses

p. 17 TREACHEROUS TRAINS

FIVE-MINUTE CHALLENGE
267 mph, Shanghai

p. 20 SILLY STAMP SNAP

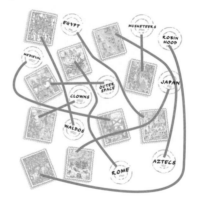

p. 21 DOG'S DINNER

ON YOUR BARKS, GET SET, GO! MY PALS AND I ARE CHASING OUR FAVORITE THINGS: SAUSAGES, BONES, AND CATS!

FIVE-MINUTE CHALLENGE
Turn the page and find an accordion

p. 24 **TO THE TAIL END**

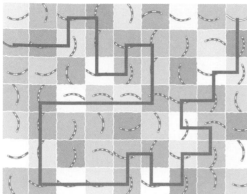

p. 27 **BULL'S-EYE!**

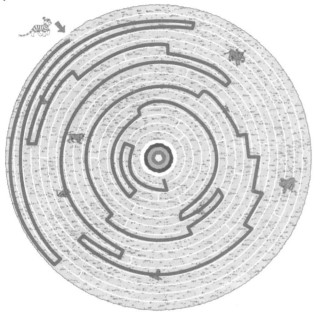

p. 28 **FLOWER POWER**

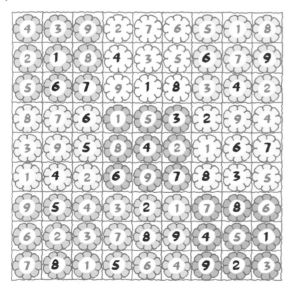

p. 29 **FRUIT PUNCH**

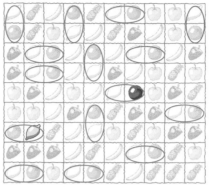

FIVE-MINUTE CHALLENGE
strawberry banana; orange mango; cherry apple

p. 30 **BALLOON BINGO**

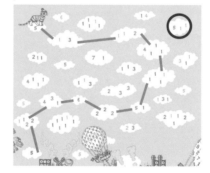

p. 31 **NUMBER CRUNCHING**

MORE THINGS TO FIND
The circled cloud has the highest value.

p. 32 **UP IN THE CLOUDS**

p. 36 WORD LADDERS

Here are some possible solutions:
HAT, HAY, HEY, KEY
MALT, SALT, SALE, SAME, GAME

FIVE-MINUTE CHALLENGE
WOW, NOW, NOT, DOT
SONG, SING, KING, KIND, FIND

pp. 38–39 TERRIFIC TITLES

FIVE-MINUTE CHALLENGE
Cinderella

pp. 40–41 TINSELTOWN

FIVE-MINUTE CHALLENGE
Darth Vader; Bo Peep; Kermit

p. 54 WHAT A CATCH!

p. 55 SEA SILHOUETTES

FIVE-MINUTE CHALLENGE
five towels; a beach-ball; two cameras

p. 56 MESSAGE IN A BOTTLE

Some options include: SCUBA DIVE; DECK
CHAIR; SWIMSUIT; SUITCASE; SUNBATHING;
SURFBOARD; SWIM CAP

FIVE-MINUTE CHALLENGE
DECK CHAIR; SUN CAP; SCUBA DIVE; SUIT
CASE.

p. 57 FISHING NET SETS

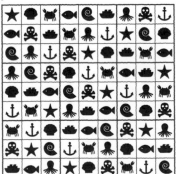

FIVE-MINUTE CHALLENGE
Fish have no bones

p. 58 SEASHELLS GALORE

FIVE-MINUTE CHALLENGE
the sea; C; they are both in the middle of waTer

p. 59 GONE FISHING

FIVE-MINUTE CHALLENGE
A red-striped fish is missing.

p. 62 BLOWING BUBBLES

mermaid; seaweed; turtle; snorkel; squid; yacht;
island; shark; reef; crab; tide

p. 64 SEA SETS

MORE THINGS TO DO
fsh; ten-tickles

p. 66 SOMETHING FISHY

p. 67 SNAKY SEARCH

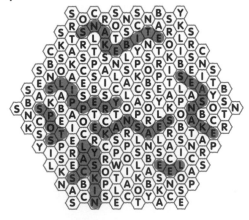

p. 77 SKULL AND CROSSWORD

p. 79 PIECES OF EIGHT
FIVE-MINUTE CHALLENGE
Blackbeard Bay; Crocodile Cove; Long John Lake

p. 88 GREAT GUIDEBOOKS

p. 89 PLAY BALL

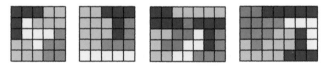

p. 91 DINORAMA
FIVE-MINUTE CHALLENGE
TRICERATOPS; PTERODACTYL; DIPLODOCUS

p. 92 TRUTH OR TAILS?
1. True; 2. False: A dinosaur scientist is called a paleontologist; 3. True; 4. True: TRICERATOPS; 5. True; 6. True; 7. True; 8. False: It had two wings; 9. False: It had a very long neck; 10. False: Dinosaurs actually lived until sixty-five million years ago. Wow!

ONE MORE THING!
stegosaurus

p. 93 WOOF'S WORD WHEEL
It's as hard as rock – stone; *Woof's favorite thing – bone; Used to sniff* – nose; *Heads, shoulders, knees and* – toes; *Woof is one of these* – dog

p. 97 CAVE LIFE QUIZ
1. Tools were made of stone 2. Hunted and gathered food 3. Paintings of animals 4. Bears & lions 5. Elephants 6. Rhinos & mammoths 7. Fire 8. Pigs 9. Clothes & tools 10. Spears

p. 98 WRITE LIKE AN EGYPTIAN
Top: Find a crocodile face! Then find another crocodile elsewhere in this book! Make it snappy!

p. 99 PYRAMID PUZZLE

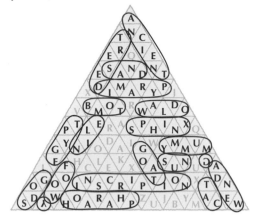

p. 101 VERUM AUT FALSUM?
1. False; 2. True; 3. True; 4. False; 5. True; 6. False; 7. True; 8. True; 9. True; 10. False

pp. 102–103 TRUTH OR TAILS?
FIVE-MINUTE CHALLENGE
Jupiter: Thunder; Venus: Love; Minerva: Wisdom; Mars: War; Mercury: Travel; Diana: Hunting; Neptune: Seas

p. 104 BUILDING BLOCKS

p. 108 NORSE CODE
Map in hand for pirate gold

FIVE-MINUTE CHALLENGE
Find the Viking ships on another page

pp. 114–115 COUNT OF THE CASTLE
FIVE-MINUTE CHALLENGE
knight; jester; apothecary

p. 116 WORD CASTLE

p. 122 DIGGING FOR GOLD

FIVE-MINUTE CHALLENGE
c / three

p. 123 MIX-UP MADNESS

p. 132 DRAGON MEDAL MAYHEM

Hansel Dusty: The Treasure Hunt Race; Sunny-Side-Up Sid: The Upside-Down Race; Edwina Sharp: The Sword-Fighting Race; Cornelius Compass: The Navigation Race; Count Bill Crunch: The Number Crunching Race; Bump-in-the-Night Bernie: The Night-Fright Race; Snoozy Van Winkle: The Forty Winks Race

FIVE-MINUTE CHALLENGE
The future; a map; a stamp

p. 134 FLYING HIGH
FIVE-MINUTE CHALLENGE
unicorn; griffin; sphinx

p. 135 SPELL-TACULAR!

Magic makes much mayhem

p. 138 GENIE-OUS!

p. 139 TERRIFIC TRAVELS

4 red birds; 7 custard pies; 5 pairs of sunglasses; 9 green hoods; 7 yellow fish; 9 hats with feathers; 8 mustaches.

p. 143 STARS AND STRIPES
The path marked in yellow leads to Waldo's golden star.

p. 144 SHIELDS AND STAVES

p. 145 GIANT GAME

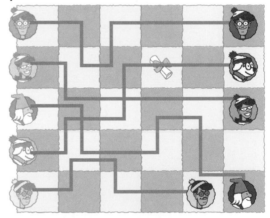

p. 152 TOP FIENDS

Warty Gretel   Heave Ho Henry   Captain Cutlass   Hungry Growler

p. 153 **SWAMPY SWIRL**

You've obviously learned some sneaky spying skills to be able to decode my message – I've taught you well. Enter my swamp if you dare. Squelch! Yuck! Phew! What a stink! Now, see if you can find me on the page. I'm the one sipping an ice-cold drink while all my best striped accomplices cause chaos. Top notch!

p. 156 **WHICH WITCH IS WHICH?**

1. Mystic Martha plays a brilliant broom tune.
2. Noisy Norma likes to wake the dead.
3. Wicked Wartie wears a cloak at night, and its color rhymes with fright.
4. Tangle Toes Tina trips everywhere she goes.
5. Moorb Hctiw rides her broom in a peculiar way.

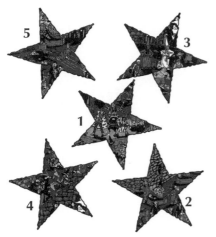

p. 157 **CONNECT THE BONES**

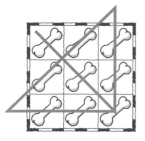

FIVE-MINUTE CHALLENGE

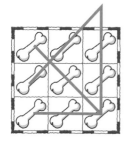

p. 158 **BIRD SEARCH WORD SEARCH**

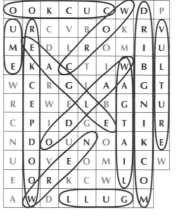

FIVE-MINUTE CHALLENGE

Sparrow Owl Hawk Warbler Swan

p. 162 **SNAKING WORDS**

1. Viking; 2. Musketeer; 3. Skull-and-crossbones

p. 166 **PLANET HOP**

FIVE-MINUTE CHALLENGE

Mars is known as the red planet; Jupiter is the fastest-spinning planet; Saturn has 62 moons; a year on Mercury is 88 years in Earth time

p. 168 **MOON MAZE MAYHEM**

p. 169 MOON MUDDLE

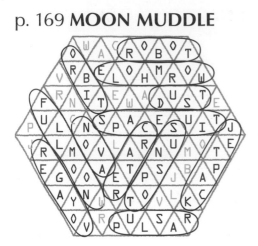

p. 170 TELEPORTATION TANGLE

p. 175 WANDERING LINES

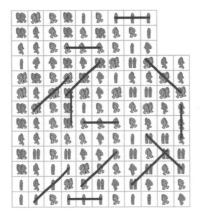

p. 176 MAKING CONTACT

Panel 1: Greetings, clever earthlings! Unscramble these codes below.

Panel 2: Find a planet with seven red aliens standing on it. It's not far away!

Panel 3: Locate five red-hooded monks shooting fire. A ship has crash-landed on that page!

p. 177 WORD WORLDS

1. Extraterrestrial 2. Universe 3. Space 4. Moon 5. Satellite 6. Astronaut 7. Mars 8. Sun 9. Twinkle 10. Telescope 11. Comet 12. Milky Way

FIVE-MINUTE CHALLENGE
Sputnik; Apollo Eleven; Curiosity Rover

p. 178 HALF ALIEN, HALF . . .

p. 180 SPACE MAIL

Answers counterclockwise from top left

p. 186 WHO'S WHO?

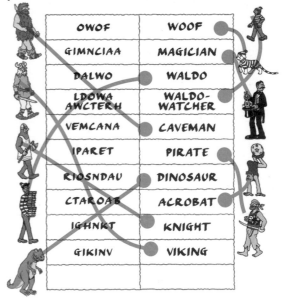

OWOF	WOOF
GIMNCIAA	MAGICIAN
DALWO	WALDO
LDOWA AWCTERH	WALDO-WATCHER
VEMCANA	CAVEMAN
IPARET	PIRATE
RIOSNDAU	DINOSAUR
CTAROAB	ACROBAT
IGHNKT	KNIGHT
GIKINV	VIKING

p. 187 CAKE-TASTROPHE

sugar; butter; eggs; flour; vanilla extract; baking powder

FIVE-MINUTE CHALLENGE
chocolate; cream; cinnamon

pp. 188–189 WHO DONUT?

Odlaw stole the cake! He said he was out all morning, but Woof and Wizard Whitebeard both saw him. And there's no mail on Sundays!